ISBN: 979-8533882866

Line Editing and Proofing: Jamie from Holmes Edits

Cover: Covers by Juan

Character Art: @kalynne_art on Instagram

WOLF TAKEN

LUNA MARKED BOOK TWO

HEATHER RENEE

DEDICATION

For Kel.

Thanks for believing in me and reminding me to whip my hair back and forth.

CONTENTS

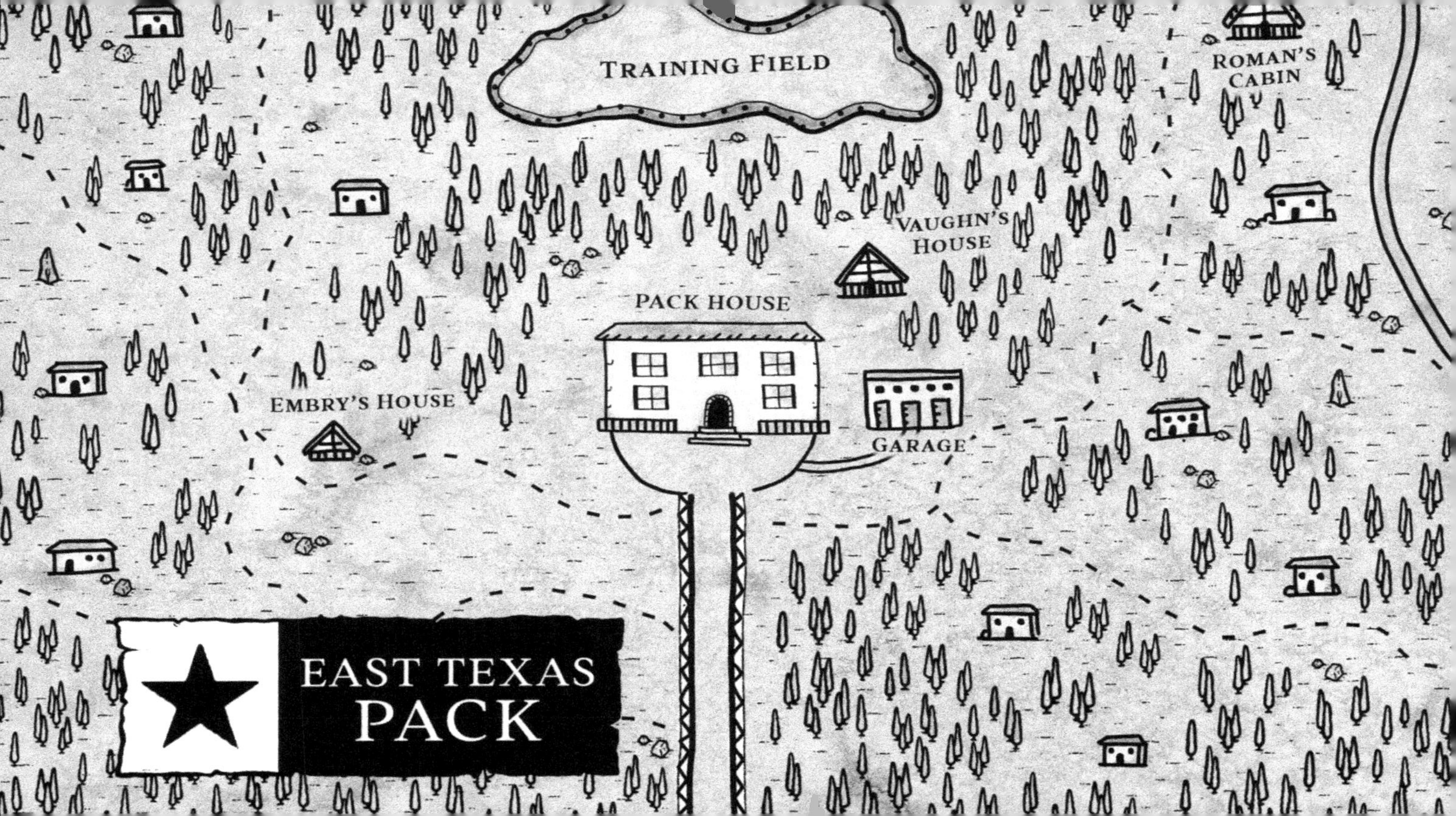

TRAINING FIELD
ROMAN'S CABIN
VAUGHN'S HOUSE
PACK HOUSE
EMBRY'S HOUSE
GARAGE
EAST TEXAS PACK

1

CAIT

Thirst and agony. Those were my first thoughts as I tried to recall what had happened. My skin itched nearly as badly as my eyes burned, and I had no idea how long I'd been unconscious. It was the first moment of clarity I could remember since not-Serene had yanked me into oblivion.

Before I dared to move, I listened carefully for any sounds. Without thought, I sniffed the air, which should have weirded me out, but it seemed like the right thing to do. Decay of some sort filtered through my senses as I tried not to gag and draw unwanted attention.

I blinked rapidly, trying to ignore the ache in my eyes, and took in the room. Dirt walls surrounded me, a tin bucket was about five feet to my left, and there was a chair across from me. Empty.

The only visible light cascaded across the barren room from what I assumed to be an exit, but I didn't bother to worry about that. At least not yet. I was severely dehydrated and hungry as hell, meaning I had very little strength and I had to choose my moves carefully.

Sitting and waiting for someone to return wasn't an option I was fond of. I closed my eyes and focused on my energy. It had been acting up in the forest before not-Serene had taken me. I hadn't been able to use my abilities, and nothing seemed to improve since I'd been knocked out.

Only the tiniest of flutters moved through me, and I wanted badly to see my mark, but that wasn't going to happen with my hands secured behind my back.

I shifted my wrists around, hoping to find some slack in the coarse rope, but I only managed to scrape my skin.

Taking another look around, I found dirt and more dirt and nothing helpful. My anger rose, and a part of me hoped that the strong emotion was what I needed to tap into whatever magic I'd had, but even as I drew on the feelings, nothing inside me changed.

Maybe the witch had figured out how to take the power from me while I'd been unaware. That was a strong possibility, and I wasn't sure how I felt about that.

Did any of it matter? Even if I was no longer supernatural, I highly doubted I was making it out of this hole-in-the-ground alive. Whoever had taken me probably planned to bury my ass inside once they were done with me.

A whistling sounded from above and I froze. In the

time I'd been awake, I'd found nothing to better my situation. I wasn't ready to face my captor, but I also needed to know who I was up against.

Maybe there would be more than one person and they'd talk in front of me if they thought I was still passed out. Yes, that was as good of a plan as any.

I let my head hang down until my chin touched my chest, then evened my breathing, which became harder once the aroma of something delicious filtered through my nose. Saliva filled my mouth, and I swallowed it down, cringing as my throat ached from the action.

"Quit the games, mutt. Your racing heart gave you away before I even came down here," a familiar voice said right before rough fingers gripped my chin. "I'm so glad you're awake, *Julie*."

Kyle, Roman's cousin, stared me down with dark russet eyes and tousled obsidian hair as I sneered at him. He was just as smug as he'd been the only other time I'd seen him, and I badly wanted to pummel the smirk off his face.

"Oh, wait. It's not Julie, is it?" Kyle's voice lowered. "It's *Cait*."

Tiny droplets of spit landed on my cheek as he glowered at me.

My eyes darted to his other hand, the one not trying to rip my chin off. The warmth of what I was beginning to believe was stew was calling me, and my stomach's rumble echoed through the room.

"Ah, yes. You're probably hungry, little freak. Possibly even a bit parched?" Kyle released me with a shove, causing the chair legs to wobble, and pulled a bottle of water from his back pocket.

I tried to lean forward, but the ropes kept me strapped tightly to the metal chair beneath me. "What do you want?"

"I want to know who, and what, you are. I want to know how Roman found you and what his plans are for you. My grandfather seems to think the two of you are connected, but I don't agree. Though, it is curious that he's tearing apart Texas to get you back." Kyle set the soup down and cracked open the water before taking a slow pull of the cool liquid I so badly needed. "Maybe if you tell me something interesting, I'll share what I've brought."

Embry and Roman hadn't wanted Kyle to know who I was, but I was going to die without water soon. Guessing from my rapid breathing, lightheadedness, and chills, it had been several days without any sort of hydration. A normal human could usually only last a few days this way, but I wasn't sure how things might have changed for me after I got the mark.

Once Kyle was done tempting me with the water, he sauntered closer, rubbing a hand over his hair. "So, what's it going to be, Cait? Will you continue being stubborn only to die, or cooperate so you can live?"

He was making it sound like this wasn't our first conversation, and I didn't like not remembering the previous times he'd likely been down here with me.

"How do I know you won't kill me anyway?" I

asked, trying to buy time in order to think of lies for his questions.

"You don't, but you also don't have much of a choice. Stakes are high, and it's time to place your bet. I'm bored and ready to move on." Kyle glanced over his shoulder and yawned as if trying to prove his point further.

"I'm Cait, as you've already figured out, and I'm human," I said.

Before I could think about the other questions, Kyle's palm struck my cheek so hard that my neck cracked from the impact. I hissed in pain.

"Don't lie to me. You're not fae *or* human. I thought maybe both, but that's not right, either. Callista couldn't take your magic. Why?"

"Fuck. You," I spat, and blood splattered across my thighs as I emphasized my words. I also hadn't missed the name I assumed belonged to the witch.

I was so thirsty that I was tempted to swallow the remaining blood down in a pathetic attempt to give my throat some relief. Instead of giving in to desperation, I spit the rest of the crimson onto the ground.

Kyle gripped my hair, yanked my head back, and exposed my neck. His right hand came up with claws. "Do you not understand how easily I could end your insignificant life?"

"If you wanted me dead, I'd already be a rotting corpse. You need me." I strained to get the words out, trying to ignore the anguish and fire searing down my throat from the effort to speak.

He shoved me back hard enough that my chair teetered even more than before, giving him the incentive to kick it over. I had no way to brace myself and tensed for the impact as my head rocked against the back of the chair. Dirt puffed up around me, and my vision wavered, but I refused to black out with Kyle still around.

"What is going on down here?" a deep male voice bellowed.

"I'm just having a little chat with our guest, Alpha," Kyle said proudly, lifting his chin a little higher in the air.

The newcomer was the male version of Ramona, and I knew he had to be Cohen. His skin was tanner and hair more grey than blond, but the umber eyes, strong cheekbones, and defined nose were all identical to the alpha female I wished was here.

You're not alone, Cait. Just stay strong, a feminine voice sounded through my mind.

Holy mother-freaking shit.

It took every effort not to lose my cool in front of Cohen and Kyle as I tried to figure out who was in my head. I knew wolves could communicate telepathically, but I wasn't a wolf, right? I couldn't even sense the pulsing from my mark any longer. The only logical explanation was that the dehydration was causing me to go crazy.

You're not crazy. She paused, and some of my pain eased. *I can't stay present. Just trust this is almost over.* The woman's voice faded away, and a sense of tranquility settled over me as Cohen righted my chair, brushing the dirt and hair from my face.

His hands were cold, just as I assumed his heart to be. Yet, it took a bit of effort not to let my guard down when he stared at me compassionately like Ramona had so often done during our training sessions.

"I'm sorry, Cait. My nephew doesn't have the best hospitality. I'm Cohen, AAlpha to the West Texas pack." He stepped back, awaiting my reply.

"I'd like to leave," I said, ignoring the stray tears that had leaked out while I'd been mentally ignoring the aching roar of pain from hitting my head.

Cohen leaned down low until we were eye level. "You can do that just as soon as you tell us why my grandson has such an interest in you. My witch Callista told me what she discovered, but I'm having a hard time believing she understands the situation."

"He told me once he preferred brunettes to blondes. Maybe it's just my hair. Would you like me to change the color, so he'll leave me alone?" My words were a total lie, but I wasn't sure what else to do. Even though it sounded like he was aware of my bond to Roman, I wasn't giving that information freely.

Cohen had tried to have Roman killed by sending one of his wolves to challenge his own grandson for a position he had no right to take. If they had confirmation of my connection to Roman, or what I was, I didn't want to think about what they might do to me.

Cohen reached back and grabbed the water from the

other chair. At first, I assumed he was only going to tease me with it like Kyle had, but then his soft fingers squeezed my cracked lips open and the ice-cold liquid branded its way down my throat.

I greedily gulped down as much as I could, enjoying as some of the coolness dribbled down my neck, soaking my dirtied tank top. Just because we weren't under the sun, didn't mean it wasn't hot as Hades in the underground bunker.

"Now, not too much or you'll make yourself sick. How about some food next?" Cohen turned to Kyle. "Untie her."

"Are you sure about that?" Kyle questioned.

Cohen's kind eyes turned murderous in an instant, and his fingers wrapped around Kyle's throat. "Do you doubt my capability to keep one measly girl where I want her without the assistance of restraints?"

"No, Alpha," Kyle gargled.

Cohen shoved Kyle away. "Good. Now, do as you're told."

Kyle cowered and stumbled his way toward me. His movements were jerky, causing me further pain that I kept to myself. I didn't need the two of them fighting and me getting caught in the crosshairs.

No, I needed to stay focused and figure out what Cohen's game was.

Once I was untied, I slowly pulled my arms in front of me, choosing not to stand. I had a feeling I was too weak to do so and didn't want them to see me falter. Red welts covered my wrists, and the mark I'd grown used to seeing was nearly gone. If I'd never known it was there, I wouldn't have even recognized the hazy image of the crescent moon.

Cohen handed me the now-lukewarm soup. Kyle hadn't bothered to bring a spoon with him, but I didn't care. I used the bit of strength those gulps of water had given me and tilted the glass bowl up to my lips. I groaned while the brothy taste coated my tongue, and as much as I wanted to choke every ounce of the soup down, I took my time. Cohen had been right about one thing—I didn't need to make myself sick by overindulging too soon.

"Now that you're a bit more comfortable, I'm wondering if you wouldn't mind having a little chat with me, Cait." Cohen took a seat in the chair across from me as Kyle sulked away to lean against the back wall.

"Sure. How about we start with what day it is? Maybe the time? Or, even better, how about why you took me?" I asked.

Cohen grinned as his eyes darkened. "I can see how you caught the attention of my grandson. You have fire in you. I wonder where that comes from."

"From my very human mother who gave birth to me," I retorted.

He raised a brow. "Interesting."

"What is?" I asked.

"You're telling the truth," Cohen replied.

I scoffed. "Of course, I am. I already told Kyle that I'm human. I'm nothing special. You got the wrong girl if you were expecting anything different."

Cohen leaned forward, an excitement in his demeanor I'd yet to see. "Now, you just might believe that, but *I* know you're wrong."

"Yeah? How's that?" I didn't like Cohen thinking he knew things about me that I didn't.

"Do you remember when you met Kyle? He left you with a parting gift that was meant for my daughter. One that should have ended your life then, but yet, here you sit—alive and well. A human wouldn't have survived a spell crafted to kill a shifter."

Blood rushed from my face as I tried not to be overwhelmed by Cohen's words. Instead, I focused on memories of when Kyle had been at the pack and our brief time together. He'd grabbed on to me when we first ran into each other. He paid a lot of attention to me, but I couldn't remember any kind of "parting gift" that Cohen spoke of.

I'd been sick after meeting Kyle, but it had been nothing more than the flu. Or at least I'd thought so.

"I can see you trying to figure it out, but that's not why we're here. You're hiding something, and I'm going to figure out what. The only thing you need to worry about is how big of a role I play in doing so." Cohen smiled softly at me, but malice bled from his words.

I didn't want him to have anything to do with me, in any capacity.

"Listen, I don't know what you want from me. I was

born human. I was raised human. I don't have a wolf. I'm nothing special."

Cohen stood and walked closer before patting my head. "You're right. All of that is true to an extent, and I'm also aware that you're choosing your words very carefully. You're smarter than I was hoping for, but I assure you that no amount of wit is going to keep your thoughts safe for long. Rest up, Cait. We're only just getting started."

He strode toward the exit, pushing Kyle ahead of him, then turned back to me. "There will be a half-dozen wolves who bite first and ask questions second, circling above. I wouldn't advise trying to escape."

I glared at the alpha's retreating form and, for the first time, wished like hell I still had my magic.

2

ROMAN

Blood and rage consumed me as I hunted the lands for Cait. The other half of my soul. My reason for existing. I hadn't thought losing her would ruin me so completely, but that was when I assumed I'd be able to keep an eye on her from afar after she rejected me.

This was my punishment for presuming and not fighting harder. I'd been weak and too patient. Two things I wouldn't be any longer.

Cait's presence was hidden from me. The floral, citrus, and mint scent that was so uniquely hers was nowhere to be found, but I wasn't giving up.

I'd find my mate and rip out the throat of whoever dared to take her from me.

The last three days had been spent tearing through Texas, trying to find Cait. Embry had these instances when she could sense when something was right, and she assured me that when her intuition said Cait was still in Texas, she had full confidence it was right.

It was hard to trust Embry's instinct when it came to Cait's life, but my wolf agreed with her, and I wouldn't argue with him. Not when I knew he was just as invested in finding our mate as I was.

We'd interrogated our own packs, a coven we stumbled upon, and a few supernaturals passing through. None of them had seen or even heard of Cait, not that I gave them a lot of information. Telling the wrong people she was Luna Marked—or even my mate—wasn't an option I was desperate enough to use. If I did, more than just me and my guards would be looking for her.

The only thing that had kept me moderately sane during my search were the infuriating yet satisfying moments when those passing through refused to even consider answering my questions with words and chose more violent options.

That was when I allowed my wolf to take action and we let out mere fragments of the wrath we were barely managing to contain.

I'd never been particularly vicious, but these were no ordinary times, and keeping my moral compass at the forefront was the least of my priorities. I'd made it known that nothing was off limits when it came to getting Cait back, not even sneaking onto my grandfather's land, wondering if he'd stooped low enough to have anything to do with taking my mate.

My wolf's legs picked up the pace at that thought as the moon shone down on us, paws practically flying over the ground as we thought of nothing other than finding Cait. If I had anything to say about it, the witch that had stolen her would die a slow and excruciating death, and I eagerly awaited the moment my teeth sank into the witch's neck—dreamed of it even.

Nothing would save that woman from my fury, whoever she was.

Are you coming home today? Vaughn's voice cut through my dark thoughts.

I don't know.

I'll join you then, he offered.

Vaughn had gone back to the pack after I'd nearly broken his arm. In my defense, it had only been two days since losing Cait when he'd pushed me a little too far with his sense of humor. By then, my sanity slipped enough that I'd seen red within a second of him laughing at his own joke.

After Vaughn had agreed to give me some space, he'd taken off but left wolves to trail me as if I wouldn't notice. As long as they stayed out of my way, I didn't waste my energy dealing with them.

I'm fine on my own, I grumbled to Vaughn as my wolf led us through the woods on the north side of my grandfather's land.

Being in their territory without his permission could get me killed, but I didn't care. I wouldn't leave a single mile of ground unturned until I found my Cait.

You're walking a dangerous line, Roman. One you might not be able to come back from as an alpha, Vaughn warned.

Do you think I fucking care about being alpha right now?

None of that matters without Cait. I will find her, no matter the cost.

Vaughn's sigh echoed through my head before I cut the connection off and came to a stop about a mile from the pack house.

I couldn't sense any magic, but I didn't know the witch that had vanished with my mate. I didn't know what she was capable of or how powerful she might be.

All I knew was the witch had something that wasn't hers.

Ours, my wolf snarled.

He hadn't been speaking to me much since we lost Cait. His mind was solely focused on tracking our mate, and I had no objections to that.

As we crept closer to the main house where I could sense plenty of wolves, a presence I hadn't expected pressed against my mind.

Serene?

You need to get back here. Beatrix is on her way. She's your only hope in locating Cait.

When did you wake up? I asked, hesitating to turn around.

I'd saved coming to this pack last for several reasons, one of them being that a small part of me hoped my grandfather couldn't hate me enough to commit the worst possible action against another wolf. Harming one's mate was unforgivable by our council. Yet, the less emotional side of my brain knew Cohen was absolutely capable of something so vile, if he'd managed to find out what Cait was to me.

Serene's voice grew weak as she spoke again. *I don't have time to explain. Get home if you want to save your mate.*

Before I could answer, the connection ended, and my wolf was turning around.

What are you doing? We're already here. It won't take long to look around, I said.

As much as I'd love to rip some of these wolves to shreds, you're not the only reason we saved coming here for last. If we're wrong, and Cait's not here, Cohen could force the council to take action against you, which could prevent us from ever finding Cait. That was a consequence I was willing to risk when we had no other options, but Serene has now given us one. If we ignore her and fail… It's not worth it.

He was right. I didn't like the thought of turning back now, but we'd gotten nowhere during the last several days doing things our way.

If Beatrix didn't have information that could help us, then maybe she'd at least have resources we could use that wouldn't alert our wolf council. They were the last thing I needed to deal with at the moment.

If all else failed, I'd remind everyone around me why I was born to be an alpha. I'd show them the power I'd been keeping buried and was no longer opposed to using.

Nobody, and nothing, was off limits until I had Cait in my arms.

3

CAIT

The water was long gone, and I'd savored the soup—that hopefully hadn't been poisoned—for as long as I could. Once darkness fell, I assumed nobody was coming back down to my hole of doom, as I'd so named it, and I risked checking out the only way in or out.

Moonlight streamed along the bumpy walkway. Besides that, I couldn't see much more than a ladder that led above ground. My skin tingled under the light as I stretched my muscles. I didn't feel strong like I'd been when working with Embry and Ramona, but something stirred inside me for the first time since I'd woken up.

That, along with the voice I'd heard earlier, was enough to give me a bit of hope. For a little while, anyway.

Are you there... uh... ma'am? I asked, having no idea what to call the woman in my head.

There was no reply as I paced back and forth. Everything around me was quiet except the rapid beating of my heart and the tapping of my nervous fingers as they drummed against my thighs.

Sleep under the moon. You'll need all the rest you can get for what's to come. The woman's voice startled me, and I hissed.

Can't you give a girl some warning? I snapped.

No, I can't. I could hear the roll of her eyes by the sharp tone she used. *Like I said before, I can't stay long, but I need you prepared. Tomorrow is a new moon. Sleep as close to the exit as you feel comfortable, and I will be back again as soon as it's time.*

Time for what? Who are you? What is happening? I asked, barely breathing.

Silence was my only reply. The woman was gone. Again. I wasn't sure which was more frustrating: being trapped down here or having someone randomly popping into my head. Okay, that was obviously a lie, but I was ready to figure a way out of the shitty situation I'd been thrown into.

I refused to be beaten without a fight. I knew I didn't stand a chance against shifters and witches, but I'd keep trying to call on whatever power had drawn the wrong kind of attention to me. There had to be a way I could get out on my own.

Then, I was going to have a serious talk with myself. Clearly, I'd made a mistake. Likely more than one, but that was beside the point. I wasn't stubborn enough to deny I was better off staying with Embry and Roman than I was on my own. And maybe, just maybe, I needed to accept the curveball life had thrown my way instead of being so damned afraid of change.

I used to be a firm believer that everything happened for a reason. Then, my mom was taken so harshly from me. She'd been fine one day, then gone the next. I'd had no time to process the thought of life without her. It hadn't been fair. It hadn't been right. I'd had no control, and it had altered me irrevocably.

I'd let Embry in because she brought light into my life when I'd needed it most, but anyone else? I'd kept them at arm's length and made sure they never had any power to hurt me.

Being told I was bonded to Roman had been everything I'd feared the most. Instead of facing the situation head on, I'd done everything I could to push him away from me. Knowing Roman was supposed to be an instant happily-ever-after scared me, considering how much he could also hurt me if I let him get too close.

After being alone with my thoughts for the day, I was kicking myself in the ass for being such a chickenshit.

Roman had been kind and patient. He'd given me choices. He'd accepted me into his world and offered nothing other than protection, but I'd thrown it back into his face. I was officially the world's biggest asshole.

I wasn't ready to have his babies, by any means, but

if I made it out of this hole of doom alive, I was willing to get to know him better and stop fighting whatever was happening between us. We both deserved that.

Leaves crunched on the ground above me, and I slid back into the darkness, holding my breath.

A woman's voice sounded. "Everything staying quiet tonight, Felix?"

"Sure is, D. I think she's sleeping," a guy much closer replied.

"And nobody has been down there since the alpha gave orders?" she asked.

"I've been here the last four hours and haven't seen anyone."

"Good. You call me if you do."

There were a few beats of silence followed by a howl that had my skin tightening. The howls grew quieter until there was nothing but eerie silence. After a few minutes, I chanced moving back into the moonlight and lay down on the ground.

My head rested awkwardly against the dirt wall, and my eyes grew heavy. The day was finally catching up to me, but I was hesitant to let sleep claim me. I didn't want Kyle or that witch Callista to come back and mess with me while I was out of it.

Rest, young one. I will keep watch. The woman's voice was back in my head, but this time I didn't question her. She wasn't going to answer me anyway, and I needed the sleep.

Tomorrow would be a better day. All I had to do was

figure out how to get away from this pack and back to where I belonged. With Roman. And Embry.

Easy.

///

Slowly, I came to, and sunlight warmed my bruised and battered skin. Everything was already feeling heaps better than the day before, and the stirring of a slow-building energy inside me was enough to reignite the hope I'd clung to the night before.

I took in the rest of me as I got to my feet. My shirt was torn at the bottom, exposing a few inches of my stomach. Dirt covered most of me, and my hair resembled a rat's nest. Lastly, I glanced at my wrist. The mark was even lighter than the day before. My heart sank.

I needed the mark. I needed the magic it provided. I'd never try to get rid of it again, if only the damned thing got me the hell out of the hole of doom.

"Felix. How is our guest?" Cohen's voice sounded above.

"I think she just got up. She's been quiet all night, Alpha."

"Good. You're off duty. Kyle will be taking over for the day," Cohen replied, and the plummeting of my heart grew.

I was never getting out of here alive, but that didn't mean I'd go down without a fight.

Walking further back into the dirt cavern, I stood behind the chair I'd been strapped to. It was the only object big enough to do some damage if Cohen or Kyle came at me.

There was an echoing thud, followed by heavy footsteps as they came closer.

"Cait," Cohen called out, but I remained silent.

He came around the corner first, with Kyle right on his heels. "How are you feeling this morning?" Cohen asked.

"Right as rain," I replied with a fake sweetness.

"Glad to hear it. Seal the room," Cohen said.

"Huh?" I asked, but nobody responded as a heaviness settled over me.

My fingers tightened around the back of the chair until the metal groaned beneath my grip. My heart pounded frantically, and any amount of breath was hard to draw as Kyle and Cohen stared me down.

"I hate to admit it, but maybe you were right, Cohen." Callista materialized beside him, and the pressure on my body eased.

"Maybe, maybe not. Either way, we need to be sure. If we can use her to get what I want, then this will all be worth it."

"What do you want?" I asked.

Kyle laughed. "Shut it, bitch. You don't get to talk unless spoken to."

Oh, what I wouldn't give to kick that asshole in his junk, followed by a swift punch to the throat.

"Now, Kyle, it's not Cait's fault she's in this situation. She seems like a smart girl, and we need to work together. Cait, this is Callista. She's been watching you for me and reporting back. She knows that you're not happy under the thumb of Roman, that he thinks you're his mate, and that you rejected him."

I internally smacked myself. Of *course* she knew. That was how I'd been lured into the forest before Callista dragged me through a portal. Yet, even though they were aware of the truth, Cohen didn't believe it was real. I wondered what made him doubt what everyone else had been so sure about.

Cohen continued, "Denying the call of a mate isn't an easy feat. On top of that, you don't possess a wolf spirit. So, either someone has an agenda for my grandson or… Well, the 'or' doesn't concern you. What should concern you is that I'm willing to overlook the many oddities about you if you stop trying to hide what you are from me. I believe that we can be of great help to each other."

If he wanted compliant Cait, I'd happily give her to him. For now. "So, you're looking for a mutually beneficial relationship?" I asked.

He grinned. "Yes, that's exactly right."

He knew more than I'd originally thought, so I had to quit playing stupid while still keeping most things to myself. "Whatever I thought I had is gone. Maybe someone planted magic in me to trick Roman. An agenda of sorts, like you mentioned. I never felt an attachment to him, so it's possible," I said, hating myself for speaking the words.

Cohen stepped closer as Callista glared daggers at me. "I'd know if another witch was up to something."

"Cait didn't say 'witch.' She said magic," Cohen said.

He seemed to be buying what I was spitting out, so I kept on going. "I rejected being in Roman's pack, which was when I sensed things changing for me. At one point, a witch told me my energy was tied to the alpha somehow, but nobody knew how exactly the magic in me worked since I was human-born. When I officially denied Roman's offer to be his mate, the power I'd been gaining began to dissipate."

Cohen reached for my wrist, his thumb gently stroking over where my mark was fading. "Well, maybe if you accept another alpha, the magic will come back."

This particular alpha was old, his breath reeked, and there wasn't a single thing about him that drew me in. The only comforting characteristic about him was his eyes, but up close, I could see the evil stirring behind them. He was nothing like his daughter.

Callista sighed and shoved Cohen out of the way. "That's not how this works. If there is still something inside that pathetic body, I'll get it out. Though, I'm not sure it's enough to do what you need."

Cohen's hand darted out and wrapped around her throat—a move that seemed to be his favorite. "Listen here, witch. You were nothing before I found you. Don't question my plans or I'll send you right back to the shithole I pulled you from. Now, prove your worth before I run out of patience."

Callista sneered at him as sparks of magic flew off her fingers, but she didn't attack. Interesting. Cohen was stronger than I assumed any of the East Texas pack realized. At least, that was what he seemed to be working toward.

Cohen released the witch and stepped back to me. "You might not have a wolf, but I believe you will, and we're going to figure out how to make that happen. When we do, you *will* accept me as your alpha."

I bowed my head, feigning submission in hopes they'd let their guards down. "I will."

"We're all shifting together as a pack tonight for the new moon. Maybe you can join us if all goes well." Cohen spoke to the witch without looking at her. "I expect results by midnight, Callista. Don't disappoint me."

I peeked up, watching as Cohen and Kyle left me alone with my least favorite of the three of them.

Callista circled me, staying close but never touching me. "Show me how you made the fire before."

"Don't you think if I could do that still, I would have tried to use it by now?" I snapped. There was no chance of negotiating with her, so I didn't bother to play nice.

Her eyes were the same black I remembered from when she'd taken me, and her sleek platinum hair cascaded around her shoulders, ending just above her waist. There were dark marks already forming around her neck where Cohen had grabbed her, but she didn't seem to mind.

"Well, then. Let's have some fun, shall we?" she cooed right before heat slammed into my chest.

My head was thrown back, but I managed to stay upright as I reached for the chair. My fingers grasped the metal, but I wasn't close enough to really grip it before Callista was on me.

"Show me your magic," she demanded.

I kneed her in the gut and shoved her off me, but she only rolled a few inches away. Not far enough to allow me any sort of head start to get away.

She grabbed onto my wrist as I went for the chair again, and my mark flared to life. Whatever surge coursed through me burned the witch, making her let go.

"There's the magic I knew was in you. Give me that and maybe I'll take it easy on you," Callista said, eyeing her hand where there was now a crescent burn mark on her palm.

"Don't you think if I had any control over the power that I'd have been using it already?" I asked, trying to move away from her, but the witch wasn't letting me out of her grasp.

Callista reached for my hair and slammed me into the chair I'd been trying to grab. "Don't get smart with me. You're nothing more than trash. I could end you right now."

I spat blood on the ground as I got up. Screw this bitch. I was done playing her games. As I steadied myself, I let her come closer. She reached for my wrist again, but there was no surge of magic this time.

"I said give me your power!" she bellowed in my face.

"Over my dead body." I slammed my elbow into her gut and jerked my head forward until it connected with hers.

Callista staggered back as I finally got a solid grip on the chair. "You're going to pay for that," she snarled.

"You're going to kill me either way. Might as well have fun before my party's over." I grinned and lifted the chair. Energy surged inside again as I hefted the metal into the air, using every bit of strength that I had to plow my make-shift weapon into the witch.

The chair connected with her ribs, and she howled in pain. I wasted no time and ran for the exit while I had the chance. As I rounded the corner and caught sight of the ladder, the bitch was already on me. She grabbed onto my hair and sent me flying backward into the wall with one jerk.

My vision faltered, and before I knew it, I was crumpled on the ground, losing consciousness. At least I'd gone out with a fight like I wanted. Callista was bleeding from her nose and had a gash on her forehead where the chair had connected. Hopefully it would scar, and she'd have something to remember me by.

She grabbed me by the hair again, dragging me across the room. "It's time to show you what real pain is."

I'm still here with you, Cait. It's not time for you to stop living, the voice from before whispered through my mind.

Except this time, her words brought no hope. I'd accepted my fate, and I was ready. I just prayed the torture didn't last long.

4

ROMAN

My mood wasn't any better when I arrived at my pack early the next morning. None of the other wolves greeted me as I stormed through our lands, heading for Serene's cabin. Beatrix had better be there already or I was going to hunt her down next. I didn't have time for games. Cait needed me.

Just as I was ready to hop onto one of the ATVs, my mother stopped me. "Son."

"What?" I didn't want to be rude to her, but I also didn't have time for her to try to talk me down from my current mood of destruction.

"Any updates?" she asked.

"I'm sure you know more than me if you've been talking to Serene."

She nodded. "Beatrix might be obnoxious, but she has always been good to our pack. Trust her."

I grunted. "I wouldn't be here if I didn't."

"You're a strong alpha and a worthy mate. You'll

find her. Just remember, you can't do this on your own. Wolves are meant to depend on each other. We live in packs for a reason."

Wrath rose within me, and I couldn't stop the snarl that tore from my lips. "Worthy alpha? She *rejected* me."

I had to give my mother credit. She didn't back down or even flinch as I raised my voice and towered over her, breathing hard and seething. "And you're going to show Cait that she made a mistake when you kill every single person that had a part in her being taken."

I nodded, thankful she seemed to be just as furious as I was about someone taking Cait from our pack lands.

She walked away as I gripped the handlebar and took a deep breath. I was back at my own home. I needed to keep my shit together.

We can shift again, my wolf offered.

No, you ran for too many days in a row. You need to rest. It's more important for you to be ready for whatever comes next after we hear what Beatrix has to say, I replied.

My wolf settled. He knew I was right. I'd never run him as much as I had the last few days, and I didn't need him too tired when it mattered most—when we took our Cait back.

Gods, I barely knew her and yet ached for her presence. Ached to smell her addictive scent as I strolled past Embry's or to watch her practicing with her unique energy in the forest when nobody else knew I was around. The desire to wrap my arms around her and never let go was stronger than anything I'd ever felt.

Thoughts of whether she was okay or injured or even worse constantly circled through my mind, driving me nearly mad. If anything happened to Cait, I wasn't sure how I would survive. Insanity was sure to set in if my mate didn't still walk this earth.

I drove the ATV toward Serene's house, ripping up the earth as I tore through the trees at higher-than-normal speeds. As I passed Vaughn's, I thought to reach out to him, but before I could open the connection, his obsidian-colored wolf was running beside me. We nodded at each other as I continued, and I was glad to have him at my side.

We arrived at Serene's a few moments later. I was jumping off of my seat before the motor had even fully shut down. The idea of kicking in Serene's door with promises to fix it later was tempting, but she opened it before I could put my thoughts into action.

"Alpha." Serene bowed her head. The previous black bruising that marred her face from the soon-to-be-dead witch was now a dull yellow, but still fueled the fury within me, reminding me of what I'd lost.

"Where is Beatrix?" I demanded, breathing hard as my wolf begged to be released.

You're not useful when you can't communicate with those who have information we need, I reminded my wolf.

Well, then settle down so I don't feel the constant need to rip someone's throat out.

He had a point, and I took a few calming breaths.

We were one, and we needed to remain in control to best help our mate.

"I'm here, but before we have our little chat, do I need to put a protection spell around myself or are you going to be a good boy and keep those claws of yours in check?" Beatrix asked from inside the house.

Vaughn placed his hand on my shoulder. "You have my word, no harm will come to you while in our pack."

"Very well, Beta. It's your life on the line if anything does happen to me." Beatrix sauntered out into the open, taking her time as if she didn't have a care in the world. This further infuriated me, but I kept my emotions to myself. Or at least tried harder to.

"Where is my mate?" I asked.

"She's on her own path. One that's been accelerated beyond what most of you were prepared for, but certain things were necessary to prevent worse from happening," the witch answered.

"How do you know what Cait's path is?" I asked.

She sighed, taking a seat on a log bench in front of Serene's house as I paced, ignoring Vaughn's watchful eyes. "I've been on this world for longer than I care to remember. I have access to magic that most witches only dream of. I keep my nose out of places it doesn't belong, and my ancestors bless me with knowledge in return."

Her high-and-mighty attitude was the last thing I needed. I took a step toward her, and she continued.

"My coven line runs deep with a history going all the way back to the original three witches. When it benefits the greater good, our ancestors will communicate with information that is passed along as needed. This includes word about not only witches, but shifters, fae, and vampires as well."

"And what have they communicated with you?" Vaughn asked.

"That Cait can't be found until after the new moon. She has to finish her current path before she can be returned to your pack," the witch answered, and I lunged forward, stopping only centimeters from her.

Without touching her, I snarled in Beatrix's face. "Where. Is. Cait?" The new moon was tonight, but sitting idle for even an hour while I had no clue if she was okay didn't work for me.

Sparks of silver magic flickered around Beatrix. "Step back or I won't share where to find her when the time is right."

I almost denied her, but this was the closest I'd gotten to learning about what happened to Cait and I needed to think twice about challenging the witch.

"What else do you know about my mate? What path is she on?" I asked, using every effort to calm the tone of my voice.

"Cait wasn't supposed to meet you for another five years. She was going to learn about Embry first, and then wolf shifters in general at her own pace. Except the balance of magic is shifting and timelines needed to be changed. The fae had their own war, which set into motion several things, and your vacation was diverted."

"I was never supposed to be in Australia when Cait was. I'd been drawn there and had no idea why." I was irritated that I'd been controlled, but equally thankful because it had led me to Cait.

Beatrix nodded. "Correct. Cait needs you just as much as you need her, but not yet. If you save her too soon, she won't be remade into her true form."

"Remade" didn't sound like it was going to be pleasant for Cait and caused a shift to begin forcing its way through me before I could consider stopping it.

Beatrix raised her hands, sending a stream of magic into my chest and freezing my change when I was only halfway done. I was stuck between beast and man with fur covering only half my body, paws for hands, and a shit-ton of pain in my hips where my bones were attempting to transform.

"You cannot interfere. My role here is to make sure of that, and I don't fail. Not ever. So, you can either stay hideously torn between being man and wolf, or you can be a good boy and stay put. Which will it be, Alpha?"

I fought Beatrix's spell, my ire too strong for her to fully contain me. It didn't matter that she was centuries old. My need to protect my mate was no match for whatever the witch used on me.

Vaughn stepped in front of me, face rigid and determined. "Come on, Ro. I understand everything hurts, but listen to Beatrix. Trust that Cait is going to be fine, because she's not weak. She's full of original power that comes from our creator. She can take care of herself, and you'll get to be there to help hold her up when it's all over if she needs it."

Our Cait is strong, my wolf agreed.

I know, but we need her.

That is true as well, but just as I knew it was right to let her go before, I feel the witch is correct. My instincts are at war with each other, but our creator has never led us astray. If Beatrix has knowledge directly from the originals, we must trust her.

Fuck! I screamed in my head as I continued to fight against the magic holding me down. Movement in my head and hands were possible at this point, but the effort it took to make that happen damn near wiped me out.

"You're a strong and worthy alpha, Roman. You fight for those you love, but there is a time for battle, and it has not yet arrived," Beatrix added.

"Who has her?" I asked through gritted teeth as I began to transform back into man. As I did, the witch's spell loosened its hold on me.

"I will tell you when the new moon has risen. I will also send you directly to your mate through a portal. Your wait will be rewarded, but only if you heed my warnings. Those who have caused harm to Cait cannot be attacked yet, not if you want any hope of a future with her."

"What is coming?" I asked, trying to ignore the thought of "harm" coming to Cait.

"One of your fellow pack alphas wishes to control the wolves, to be the new creator and draw his power from all those beneath him. This alpha found a prophecy that led him to believe he could steal magic from the witches, fae, and vampires, then use it to take from the Moon Goddess."

"Then, why doesn't she just kill him?" Vaughn asked.

Serene came out of her house then, and I'd never even realized she'd disappeared. She was holding a leather-bound book that appeared centuries old. "She cannot take the life that she gives. It is her only rule. She can, however, lead others onto a path which might correct her mistakes. Just like anyone else, our creator is not perfect, but she is just. The Moon Goddess lives by her rules and has never deviated from them."

I grunted. "Well, maybe if she did, we wouldn't be in this mess."

"Or maybe things would only be worse. Do you wish to live your life by 'maybes'?" Beatrix challenged.

Unfortunately, the witch had a point.

I wanted to ask a million more questions, but none of the answers would help me get Cait back any quicker. I decided to leave well enough alone and turned to Vaughn. "How is the pack?"

"A united front. They all understand why you left, and Embry has been helping me to make sure we don't need to worry about anyone turning against us. She's rather scary when she wants to be," he replied.

I raised a brow. "You're just now realizing that?"

He grinned. "I'm just now understanding that her fierceness was never a front, and I should have been worried about her bite all those times I flicked shit her way."

"Where is she now?" I asked, even though I could have reached out to her myself.

Serene stepped between us, placing the book she'd brought out into my hands. "Embry is running an errand for me. Leave her be until it's time to go. In the meantime, I suggest you go somewhere quiet and read this."

My fingers brushed over the cover, but there was no title I could find. "What is it?"

"Original text about the Moon Goddess that might help you tolerate what is happening if you can focus long enough to read."

"How long have you had this?" I asked sharply.

"Long enough. Now, Beatrix and I still have things to discuss. Leave us be until tonight. You won't get anything else out of us until then," Serene said as she turned her back on me.

Brave wolf given my current state, but then again, I'd never hurt one of my own. Not unless they truly deserved my wrath. Unfortunately for my rage, keeping Cait on a path that brought her back to me, even if it wasn't *when* I wanted, didn't justify punishment.

I gave Vaughn my attention again. "Is Sam back yet?"

"No, we haven't heard from her. Did she say how long she'd be gone this time?" he asked.

I shook my head. "I was just hoping she'd be able to

come with us, given we have no idea what we're going up against when we get Cait."

"Either way, we can handle it," Vaughn replied, and I knew he was right.

Except, I had a feeling things were only going to get more complicated once I had my mate back, and I'd need everyone I trusted at my side.

5

CAIT

Never before had I been so filled with rage, yet felt utterly pathetic at the same time. With every strike Callista hit me with, I grew increasingly hot on the inside. Power stirred inside me, begging to be unleashed, but nothing ever happened.

No flames. No energy. Just a nothingness slathered in frustration.

"Come on, mutt. If you don't give me something, I'll only torture you longer. I mean, either way, I get something out of it, but I'd rather have your magic than the pleasure of drawing out your death. So, how about we make a deal? You give me what I want, and I'll show you some mercy."

"Screw…you," I mumbled before wiping blood off my chin and flicking it to the dirt floor of my temporary prison.

Callista's magic traveled over my skin, soft at first, giving me a false sense of security—just like the first hundred times—before piercing deeper, making my blood boil, my bones crack, and my skin melt away.

Okay, none of that *actually* happened, but it sure the hell seemed like it as the bitch circled and taunted me.

The woman whose voice had been in my head, almost giving me hope, was nowhere to be found when I needed her most. I'd screamed for her, begged to have access to my energy, but nothing changed inside me other than the amount of pain I received. No, that bit only continued to increase.

Cohen and Kyle had made appearances throughout the hours I'd been tortured, but neither of them had spoken to me while Callista did her best to shatter my very existence, or whatever it was she was trying to do.

The witch's fingers squeezed my neck, her nails digging into my skin while my backside was pressed into the earth wall. "You have five minutes to give me what I want," she hissed into my ear.

All I took from that was I had mere moments to live, because clearly, I wasn't able to access the damned Luna Mark energy anymore. So, I did what any reasonable person would do when their options had run out.

I rammed my head into her face as hard as I was capable of.

Her cold eyes leered at me, but she didn't say anything. Instead, she took a few steps back and headed toward the exit of my hole of doom.

She breathed deeply, relaxing her body as she closed her eyes and tilted her head up briefly. The woman was out of her damned mind, and I was ready for her to finish this. Torture was *not* my idea of foreplay.

If there was any hope of someone finding me, I was sure they'd have done so by now. I was on my own, and I wasn't strong enough to beat a supernatural, not in my current state.

Callista sauntered back over to me, keeping a slight distance between us. "My ancestors tell me you're special, that I should keep you alive. But I've broken you in every way possible except finding those you love and bringing them here to taunt you with. Though, you only have one person, right? Your heart is too cold to take the mate offered to you."

She said that last bit with disgust, as if I'd insulted her by my choice, which surprised me.

"You're right. I prefer to be on my own. Would I be sad if you hurt Embry? Of course. But it doesn't change anything. If you didn't notice, I'm selfish. I value my life more than hers, and no matter how many times you bring me to the brink of death or threaten people I know, nothing will work. I don't know what else to tell you. Whatever I had in me is gone. I'm not the one you need. Not anymore."

Only a portion of my words were true. I would die for Embry without a second thought, but I wholeheartedly believed in the latter of my words. If I was something special, I should have been able to defend myself. The Luna Mark was a joke. One big laugh supernaturals could have over the poor pitiful human.

I was being harsh, but I was on a roller coaster, only leading to one place: my death. Knowing that, I covered up my fears with anger and did what I needed to in order to process what was coming. Nobody could fault me for that.

"Sadly, I'm beginning to believe you're right, which means you're worthless and I get to kill you. Cohen won't be happy about that, but he doesn't understand magic like I do. I'm wasting mine on you and I'm done," Callista said and sighed.

She opened a portal with one hand and reached for me with the other. I stumbled back into the metal chair that had been used to beat me more than once throughout the day. I knew I'd only have one more chance to go out with a bang, and I badly wanted to leave the bitch with as many scars as possible to remember me by.

When Callista failed to grab hold of me, she huffed in irritation before finishing the portal, then sent an electric current through my chest with a wave of her hand, causing me to crash to the ground.

"Get on your feet. I'm not carrying you," she snapped, as if I'd ended up there on purpose.

My fingers gripped the warm metal of the chair I'd just been occupying, and an idea came to me. I barely had enough strength in me, but I managed to lift the chair while she turned to check the portal. She began to look back as I groaned from the effort my movements took, but the rough metal edge of the chair leg raked across her cheek before she could do anything to stop me.

I didn't stop there, either. No, I told myself I'd go down swinging and, while I'd fought back several times already, I had just a bit more left in me to give it one more go.

I dropped the chair and wrapped my arms around her waist as I shoved us through her portal. We toppled over onto dead grass, and I rolled over with Callista still in my grasp.

Grabbing a fistful of her hair, I yanked her head back with my left hand and punched her in the throat with my right. All my life I'd wanted to throat-punch someone who deserved it, and I smiled that I'd at least made that happen before time ran out.

Callista roared in my face, the shock of my actions no longer taking effect. "I'm done with you!"

She threw me off, and I landed on my back, hitting my head on a wooden log. There was nothing left in me to fight her, but I still grinned at her bloodied face and bruising neck.

Without another word, she jumped on top of me, landing on my stomach. She pinned my arms down with her legs and mumbled words I didn't understand.

Her hands pressed over my forehead and chest, burning my skin wherever she touched. My jaw clenched, fighting off the scream that so badly wanted to rip from my lungs.

"Hurts, doesn't it?" Callista smirked.

I decided to give one more go at pissing her off and

lifted my knees as hard and fast as I could, jamming them into her lower back. She lost her hold on my chest as she tumbled forward, but that only made the palm over my forehead press down harder.

No longer could I hold in the screams as she burned me from the inside out. My body began to flail underneath her, and I had no control over my movements as my insides felt like they were being shredded by a cheese grater. A very dull one at that.

My vision blurred while a numbness finally set in. This was it. I was going to die. Never again would I see my best friend. I'd never get the chance to tell Roman I was sorry for being so damned stubborn, and I'd never understand why all of this happened.

Callista raised her hand, and I thought maybe the worst of it was over—that I'd get to spend my last few minutes on Earth not writhing in pain.

Yeah, that was a dumb thought.

The witch's fist came down, crunching my jawbone. "Just a little something to remember me by," she mocked, then swung again, hitting the side of my skull. "And that was for being a royal waste of my time."

Her words continued as I lost consciousness and hoped like hell that whatever came next, there'd be no more pain. I could handle anything else.

////

When awareness came back, I had no idea where I was or what had happened to me. All I knew was that every muscle inside me felt like it was on fire. I tried to stretch my arms out, but I couldn't get my limbs to listen to the commands, and my eyes refused to open.

Panic set in as breathing became harder. I needed to focus on the things I could remember. I was Cait Jones. I was twenty-one years old. I lived in Aust—no, not Australia. I was back in the states. I'd met Embry.

There was an emergency and she'd flown me back, but I couldn't understand why. Was *I* the emergency? No, that wouldn't be right.

A comforting warmth settled over me, but I still couldn't move. I thought about Embry, trying to recall actually meeting her.

There was a big house on a property in the middle of nowhere. There were a lot of people and… no, that can't be. Wolves? Dogs? Yeah, it had to have been lots of dogs.

The sound of howling echoed through my head and caused my throat to burn with grief. The sorrowful call tore at my heart. Something about it was familiar. Had I gotten a dog?

Another memory trickled through, but it was distorted. All I caught was the name Roman. Maybe I had a dog named Roman? Shit, I didn't know how long I'd been out of it, but not remembering everything was not okay with me.

"Cait?" a soft voice called.

Yeah, I answered, but the word only echoed around inside my head.

"How are you feeling?" the woman asked.

I'd be better if I could actually talk out loud, I huffed. Wait. Why did it feel normal to talk to someone inside my head?

She chuckled. "You'll be able to soon, but it's not necessary. I can hear all of my children, no matter how they speak to me."

Your children? What in the actual hell is happening? You don't sound like my mother. The panic was back in full force as I fought against the darkness holding me down.

"I'm not the one you're thinking of. I'm your creator, the creator of all wolves," she said.

Wolves? I'd thought that earlier, but I'd dismissed the possibility because my mind had conjured up big, supernatural ones, not the normal forest-type I'd seen back in Oregon on occasion.

"You don't remember?" the woman asked, seeming just as confused as I was.

Before I could respond, cool hands pressed over my head. I sighed as a peacefulness took over, but it didn't last nearly as long as I would have liked.

"Callista is stronger than I'd given her credit for. She keeps many secrets, but this I can fix," the woman said confidently.

Light began to seep through the darkness holding me captive, but it was too bright. I tried to turn away but failed at every attempt. Strikes of agony slashed through my mind as thoughts attempted to break through.

"I knew you were more than a little strong-willed, but you're only hurting yourself now. Let me in," the stranger said, her voice deeper as she worked some sort of magic on me.

Then I realized the idea of magic didn't seem so farfetched, just like the mind talk. I already knew it was real, but I didn't remember how.

I needed to get my shit together. I needed to focus. The woman didn't seem to be making my situation worse, at least, I didn't think so. There was a possibility I needed to find a way to let her in until I got my sight back, then re-evaluate my options.

Taking a deep breath, I focused on calming myself and turning toward the light inside my head instead of fighting against it. The agony increased, but I buckled down and took the torture willingly.

Torture… the word echoed through my mind. I'd been through a certain amount of hell recently. As I accepted that thought as truth, memories flooded through until tears streamed down my face from mental and physical aches the images caused.

Embry was a wolf shifter. I was mated to her alpha Roman. I'd rejected him. I was a supernatural freak nobody knew what to do with.

It was no wonder I'd blocked it all out.

"Now, that's a lie and you know it," the woman said.

My eyes opened, and I knew immediately who she was. "Moon Goddess?"

She smiled, showcasing two perfect rows of teeth and plump lips most women would kill for. Her eyes were a striking silver and her hair as black as the night sky. There was an ethereal glow around her that put off pink vibes, and I itched to reach out and touch her light.

"Hello, Child. I'm Luna, the Moon Goddess." She reached out her hand to me, and because I was still on the ground and staring up at the celestial being like an idiot, I took her offered help.

Luna gave one slight tug, and I went tumbling into her. "I'm so sorry," I muttered.

She laughed, the sound resembling chimes. "I haven't been amongst my Earth walkers in some time. I forget our differences."

"Why are you here now?" I asked.

Luna reached for my wrist where the crescent moon was as dark as it had ever been. Something I remembered had nearly been nonexistent while I'd been captive.

"I gave you this mark when I shouldn't have. There was a plan for you, and someone interfered. I forced you into a life you weren't ready for. Mistakes happened. I'm here to fix those as best I can and to make sure you came back to life."

"I'm sorry. Come again? I'm *dead*?" My head whipped around. It was hot and humid, and I felt very much alive, but then again, what did I know about death. I'd never freaking died before.

"Well, you're not anymore. You've been reborn into your true self. The one you were destined for the day you were born," Luna said, seeming much too calm for my liking, considering the subject of our conversation.

"Are you saying that Callista really did kill me, and you brought me back to life?"

She nodded. "In a way, but it was more like I gave you the tools you needed to do so yourself. You're one of my strongest children, Cait. There is so much you have to learn, and while I can't be the one to teach you myself, I wanted you to hear some truths from me to help you moving forward."

Couldn't a girl die and come to life without having her world turned upside down for a second time? Apparently, not.

Luna settled herself onto a fallen tree, probably the same one I remembered my head smashing into however long ago that was. She patted the seat next to her, but I chose to perch myself on a rock opposite to her.

"Like I said, strong-willed. Some might call it stubbornness, but the walls you've built around you will keep you safe, will make you see things that others can't. Just don't forget to let those who care for you in," Luna said as I settled down.

"Like Embry?" I asked.

"Among others. Roman, for instance."

Ah, I should have known she'd bring him up. "Agreed. I shut him down before I ever really gave him a chance."

"Rightfully so, my child. You weren't ready, and neither was he. Roman thought he knew what it meant to be mated, but had you accepted the bond before you had died, the repercussions on your relationship would have been irreparable. You've come back a new person with a changed soul. The bond the two of you share would have been damaged during these transitions, causing fate to go even further off course in unfathomable ways."

Well, maybe things had worked out exactly how they were supposed to, regardless of how painful they'd been. And just maybe I wasn't such an asshole. My intuition just had a shitty way of going about doing what was right.

"So, why me? I'm still very confused on how I was swept up into all of this," I said.

Luna's eyes glowed, making me lean back. She closed and reopened them several times before the color was back to normal.

"What was that?" I asked.

"One of my children asking for help. You see, there is something much bigger at play here. Each of the supernatural species are experiencing their own hardships, and you are part of the wolves'. A key part, in fact. I've given life to many wolf shifters over the centuries, but it has been much too long since I've created a direct descendant such as yourself.

"You were born human. Your mother is exactly who you've always known, and that will never change. Your father, on the other hand, was one of my descendants from a powerful line that faded out over time. He was not a wolf shifter in the physical sense, but he did pass his lineage on to you."

I cleared my throat, not really sure how I felt about

asking my next question but went for it anyway. "You said 'he was.' Does that mean my father is dead?"

"I'm sorry. Yes, it does. After Michael met your mother, he began to struggle with his inner self. He'd left, believing it was best for you. In reality, the magic you inherited from him was stirring something inside him. I did the best I could to help him find his path, but he chose differently."

Michael… I hadn't heard anyone use his real name since I was a young child. It was odd yet comforting. I hoped my mother learned about this after she passed on and found some peace. His leaving had left scars deeper than I cared to remember.

"Thank you for telling me," I said solemnly.

"Would you like to know more before it's time for me to leave?" she asked.

My head lifted. "You can't leave me out here."

"Oh, I won't be leaving you alone. Your mate is frantic to get to you. I've asked for help holding him off so we could chat, but if you're ready to reunite with your friends, I can make that happen as well."

The word "mate" sent me down another rabbit hole. Was I ready to face Roman after what I'd done to him?

Luna was suddenly in front of me, grabbing my hands. "The thing you need to understand about wolves is that they're loyal to a fault. They will burn down cities to save the ones they care for. They love fiercely, and there isn't a thing in this world you could do that would push Roman away from you for good. Not even rejecting him. He was only willing to let you go because his wolf helped convince him it was the right choice."

I raised a brow. "And I assumed you helped his wolf do so?"

She grinned. "I might have given a little nudge. I'm sorry for what you had to go through. It was never supposed to be this way, but it is only going to help shape you into the wolf you'll need to be in order to find the freedom you so desire."

"A wolf? I really am a wolf shifter?" I asked, not understanding how that could be since I didn't feel any different than before I supposedly died and came to life.

"Why do you seem so surprised after all you've learned?" Luna asked.

"Well, this witch Beatrix thought I might be something else, or that I had more choice in what I became."

Luna nodded. "Beatrix is a wise witch, but she had her stories wrong. It wasn't time for her to know what you were then, and she assumed more than she should."

That was interesting and almost a little disappointing, along with the fact I didn't really feel any different. Maybe I wasn't what anyone thought.

"Oh, Cait. You have a magnificent wolf spirit inside you now that will guide you and be the light you need in your life. The two of you are a lot alike, actually. Roman will also be there, but a bond between mates and the connection between a shifter and their wolf is nowhere near the same. You'll see."

"When will I meet this wolf?" I wasn't eager for this to happen right away, but I was curious.

"How about now?" Luna suggested and gave me a shove off the rock.

I stumbled back, nearly falling on my ass, but managed to right myself at the last second. My mouth opened to yell at her. I didn't care if she was a goddess. I'd been pushed around too much over the last couple of days.

Except no words came out as my heartrate increased and muscles began to ache, but not in an excruciating way. No, it was as if I was standing on my tiptoes, raising my hands into the air and stretching as far as my body would allow.

My vision blurred for the briefest of seconds, then everything went dark and I began to blink rapidly. The change was instantaneous, but the moment awareness settled in, I knew I was no longer the me I'd always known.

Luna stood above me, smirking. For someone centuries old, she certainly had a mischievous side. One that I secretly enjoyed.

Hello, Cait, a sharp voice sounded.

Uh, hi?

I'm your wolf spirit, she deadpanned.

Something told me this particular spirit wasn't too happy about being thrown into a newbie shifter.

Yeah, well, maybe you shouldn't have rejected our mate.

Oh, this was going to be fun. I'd just met this… wolf? Spirit? and she already hated me. Just my luck.

Luna said it worked out how it should have, I said, trying to smooth things over. From what I already knew, she wasn't going anywhere.

We'll see.

Her attitude was smug, and I sensed she was a bit of a diva.

Do you have a name? I couldn't remember if Embry had told me about names or not.

I have something I go by, but now is not the time for that discussion.

The wolf's presence pulled back from my thoughts and I felt another replace hers.

Give her time. She's been alone for a long time while we waited for you. I promise, while there have been trying times and still more to come, everything will work out as it should, Luna said.

My wolf eyes focused on her as I nodded. There wasn't much I could do other than fight her words or trust they were true. I didn't have it in me to do the former.

Would you like to see what you look like? she asked.

Hell yes, I do.

The Moon Goddess laughed softly as she walked toward a small puddle of water. I had no idea where it had come from because nothing else appeared to be wet. She waved her hand over the pool of liquid and gestured for me to come closer.

Walking on four feet was easier than I expected. My grace seemed to come naturally, and I kept my head held high, proud to be in the form I was. Maybe that was more my wolf spirit than me, but I didn't care. I was tired of fighting what came my way. I was tired of running and constantly trying to be in control. It was time to find out what happened when I let go and trusted fate.

Glancing down at the water, I internally gasped. My wolf might have made a noise, but I ignored her and took in the purple glow around me. My fur was longer than any wolf I'd ever seen, with black undertones that turned into a deep violet color. Walking around the puddle, I got a glimpse of my whole self and nearly died when I caught sight of my tail.

It was long and flowy and absolutely magical as it swished back and forth.

This was the first time since I'd received the Luna Mark that I truly felt at peace with who I was, or more accurately, who I'd become. Maybe it was being in my wolf form that gave me the added confidence, or being reborn into an actual wolf shifter, but I was more than ready for whatever came next.

I'm going to leave you now. It's time for you to reunite with your friends. They're going to want to hunt down Cohen, Kyle, and Callista, but it is not time for that battle yet. You have more ahead that needs to come first. Trust those who offer aid and listen to your wolf. The two of you will need to rely on each other as the days pass. I won't be able to interfere again, but I will be watching, and I will be hoping for your success, Luna said.

What's coming? What do we have to prepare for? I

asked, but as the words traveled through my mind, the Moon Goddess began to dissipate before my eyes.

I was suddenly alone in a place I didn't recognize with a wolf spirit who didn't seem too fond of me. At least it was better than being dead.

A howl echoed through the night, and a shimmer appeared in the dark sky before me. I began to back up, not knowing if Callista had come back to finish her job, but the howl sounded again, closer this time, and I immediately knew who it was, as did my wolf.

Our mate.

6

CAIT

Roman zeroed in on us and wasted no time closing the distance between our wolves. My wolf took control, making her thoughts known as soon as she laid eyes on Roman.

Mate, she cooed.

Well, at least she'd be nice to him.

Roman's wolf knocked us over, and mine exposed her neck as he nipped at us.

Have some self-respect, girl, I muttered.

He's our mate. There is nothing wrong with letting him love us, she snapped.

I wasn't sure *loving* was what he was doing—more like claiming—but I let them have their moment. I'd hopefully get the chance to have my own with Roman as a man as soon as our other halves were done.

Embry appeared behind us, and my wolf snarled at her.

"Whoa, girl. I'm your friend. You've got nothing to

worry about from me," Embry said with her hands up, but not backing away.

How much do you like this female? my wolf asked.

We *like her a lot. She's our best friend. Bite her, and me and you are going to have issues,* I replied seriously.

The wolf grumbled incoherently, then gave her attention back to Roman's beast.

His grey wolf was practically foaming at the mouth as he sniffed and placed little bites all over my upper half. Or was it *her*, or even *our*, upper half? I wasn't sure how to describe myself anymore, but as the confusion settled, I wondered if I'd have bruises when I shifted back.

Serene and Beatrix stepped in next. My wolf was not pleased with all of our guests.

"We need to get back to the pack before someone finds us," Beatrix said, and I couldn't agree more. I'd prefer Callista to believe she succeeded in killing me.

Roman's wolf backed up, and mine whimpered. She was doing nothing to show we were strong, independent females, but then again, I promised to have an open mind and give this mate thing a chance. I'd do my best to follow her lead as much as I could. I had to still be me, though. I wasn't going to change everything for a man. I just wasn't capable of it.

Roman shifted back, and I began to panic. I had no idea how I was supposed to become *me* again.

He must have read the terror rolling off of me, because when Roman bent down, his cobalt eyes were bright with emotion and staring into my soul. He pressed his head against mine, digging his fingers into my fur.

"I can't ever lose you again," Roman whispered, voice rough with torture.

My heart broke for him. I'd had it bad being taken, but he'd suffered right alongside me. There was no denying how much he already cared for me.

"The first shift back is always the trickiest. Just focus on the form you want to take and will it to be," Roman said.

Are you going to fight me? I asked my wolf.

No, our mate needs you. I'll never deny him what he needs.

Her tone was superior, and I was ready to smack her down from her high horse. We needed to find common ground, because I wasn't going to live with her holier-than-thou attitude for long, but I could ignore it for the time being.

I did as Roman said and pictured my human body, focusing first on my long brunette hair and green eyes, then working my way down. I'd been a hot mess before shifting, and I silently hoped some of the wolf magic would clean me up a little.

My mind pushed everything else out as I focused. I was lost in the magic as power swirled inside me. My arms and legs felt like they were swaying in the wind—nothing like when I shifted from human to animal.

As relaxation set in, I sighed and opened my eyes to find Roman's bare back standing in front of me. Embry's snickering sounded from in front of him.

"Beatrix. Clothe her," Roman demanded.

I glanced down and nearly pissed myself. *Where are my clothes?* I screeched internally.

Smug once again, she said, *You forgot to think about them.*

Oh, that little...

Beatrix clapped her hands together and I was wearing black yoga pants and a tight tank top. Not the outfit I would have chosen, but it was better than being naked.

The witch then waved her hands and re-opened the portal. Embry jumped through first, seeming to realize that Roman was a brick wall she wasn't going to be getting through anytime soon. Serene and Beatrix went next, and I peeked around Roman.

"So, are we staying here or...?"

Ever so slowly, he turned. His eyes still had a glow about them, but there was an underlying darkness to them I'd missed before. Roman was broken, and every part of me yearned to soothe all his aches.

My hands raised and rested gently on his muscled chest. "I'm sorry, Roman."

"*You're* sorry?" He barked out a laugh, but there was nothing comforting about it. "I failed to do the only thing I was created to do. I failed *you*."

Tears sprung from my eyes, and I stepped closer to him, raising myself up onto the tips of my toes, so I could better meet his gaze. "You did no such thing. Shit happens. I just want to forget the last few days and figure out what happens next."

His hands fisted around my hips as I stared up at him. He was twice as wide as me and nearly a foot taller, and I'd never felt safer. One of his hands trailed tantalizingly slow up my ribs, moving around my arm, then cupped my neck as he lowered his forehead to mine.

We stood there, soaking each other in, enjoying the quiet of the night until a whistle cut through the silence, reminding us we weren't safe just yet.

Without asking, Roman picked me up, and cradled me to his chest. I wanted to object, but the warmth of his body was too comforting to deny.

We stepped through the portal and, surprisingly, I felt nothing as the magic flickered around us. Embry grinned widely, and I smiled back, aching to also hug my best friend. I'd had no idea if anything happened to her when I was taken, and it was more than a relief to see her in one piece.

Just as I thought Roman was going to let me down, he growled, tightened his hold, and then sprinted into the woods.

Nobody followed, and, as exhausted as I was, I couldn't deny that seeing this side of Roman was hot as hell.

My palms rested on his chest as I focused on the rapid beat of his heart. The longer I touched him, the more in sync we felt. My pulse pounded just as his did. My breathing leveled out, and everything else around us faded away.

As Roman sprinted through the trees, his eyes found

mine and didn't break contact until his bare foot made contact with the wooden door.

We were at his cabin, and a part of me was suddenly nervous. I could only think of one reason Roman would have brought me out here in his current state. We'd only known each other a couple weeks, and I'd spent most of that time fighting everything that drew me to Roman. I wasn't sure I was ready to dive right into the physical stuff.

Though, as I took a breath and met his stare again, listening to the sound of the shutting door, nothing else felt more right to me. Roman wasn't asking anything of me. He needed a moment and, if I really thought about it, so did I.

Mate, my wolf whispered.

With power swirling inside me, I knew she was right. Roman was ours. I hadn't been ready before. I hadn't understood what "mate" even meant, and I still wasn't entirely sure, but I knew enough to accept the safety Roman was offering me.

My back pressed against a wall as Roman shifted my position so that my legs wrapped around his waist. "Did she hurt you?" he asked, voice still rough.

"It was nothing I couldn't handle," I replied, wiggling against him as the nerves from just moments before gave way to the desire working its way through me.

Roman's hands trailed over my upper body as the pressure of his lower half kept me pinned to the wall. "I want to ask you for every detail so I can rip everyone to shreds who dared to touch a hair on your head, but…"

His words faded as he placed a soft kiss against my neck, breathing me in.

I knew what he meant. I'd just been beaten and killed and brought back to life. I should be a hot mess, but there was nothing I wanted more than his continued touch.

He heals us, my wolf said, and I had no reason to doubt her. Everything felt more energized and strengthened now that we were together like this.

Roman's lips moved slowly, barely touching my skin as he made his way to my face. "Cait, I know you didn't want this before, but the pull toward you… I can't fight it. I can't let you go unless that is truly what you want. Not after the last several days."

My first instinct was to pull Roman closer and never let him go. The old me would have second-guessed that, but I'd had my time to think, and I was done with it. I wanted Roman. I'd wanted him since the moment I laid eyes on him. I'd just been too damn scared to follow through with the emotions he elicited from me.

No longer did I want to live in fear. Roman was made for me, and it was time I accepted that fact. I was more than ready, and so was he.

"Don't let me go, then," I said, even though a part of me thought we should talk first. Then again, I'd just been tortured to death—literally—and a distraction in the form of a sexy muscled alpha was nothing to complain about. Nothing wrong with keeping reality away for just a little bit longer.

Without needing any further encouragement, Roman closed the distance between us. I kissed him with every bit of fear, excitement, and hesitation that I had been holding inside.

I put it all on the line, opening my mind and heart to the possibilities I'd found myself in. I'd never asked for this new life—I hadn't even known it existed—but I was ready. Finally.

Being reborn was the best thing that could have happened to me. The freeness flowing through me as Roman's tongue explored my mouth was exhilarating and enlightening.

He was gentle at first, letting me take control and set the pace, but that only lasted for so long. One of his hands fisted my hair at the base of my neck while the other gripped my ass, keeping me impossibly close to him.

He was only wearing sweatpants and, given Beatrix had dressed me in thin yoga pants, nothing was left to the imagination as his hard lines pressed exactly where I wanted them.

I rocked against him until the hand holding my hair slipped between us. A slight hesitation slithered through me, but I pushed it away, focusing only on the strength Roman was providing me with every touch he gave.

As the tips of his fingers stroked my skin, a moan I thought I'd be embarrassed about escaped from me. My head leaned back against the wall as I let Roman devour every piece of me that he wanted.

"I should let you rest, but I need you," Roman whispered against my neck.

"I need you, too. We can rest later."

I felt his grin grow against my skin as his fingers traveled lower, finding me just as eager for our reunion as he seemed to be.

"You are everything I didn't know I needed, Cait."

I wanted to reply with something equally as sweet, but words were lost on me as I rocked against his hand, finding the pleasure I hadn't known I needed, either.

Tender words continued to slip from his lips as he nipped, stroked, and treasured me, all while keeping me pinned against the wall.

My breathing increased until I couldn't contain myself anymore. Roman was taking my body to places I had never imagined, and I was here for it, digging my nails into his shoulders and enjoying the ride.

"Come for me, Kitten."

And come I did. Loud and proud.

Roman's touch never left me as I soared from his expert touch and let him continue to heighten my emotions. Once I felt moderately normal again, I reached for the band of his sweatpants, but he shook his head.

"Not now," he said.

"But you…"

"I am more than okay as long as I have you back. Plus, I'm going to need more time with you than what we have now for anything more." The spark in his eyes drew anticipation from me I didn't expect.

Damn, why had I waited so long for this?

It didn't matter now. I couldn't change the past, but I would do my best to embrace the future and the new life I'd been tossed into.

Roman's fingers caressed their way toward my wrist, turning it over until he could see my mark. The crescent shape was darker and bolder than it had ever been.

"I think it's linked to us. There is a pulse within it that calls to me," he said, stroking the mark.

"Possibly. It was nearly gone while I'd been underground," I replied.

With that one comment, Roman's mood deteriorated. "We should get back to the others and formulate a plan. We have a group ready to hunt the witch that took you."

I nodded, unsure if I should tell him that Callista wasn't working alone—that his grandfather had played an enormous part in my taking—but I decided to wait until we went back to the pack house. Then, I could tell everyone at once and only deal with the wave of anger I imagined would follow once.

Roman lowered me to the ground, cupping my cheeks once my feet hit the floor. "I'm sorry. I know you seemed okay with…what just happened. But you made a decision before, and I'd promised to respect it."

My head was shaking before he even finished speaking. "I'd made that choice prematurely. I'd been scared and overwhelmed and out of my element. I made a mistake."

Joy flowed between us at my words, not only from him and me, but my wolf as well. She'd been quiet, and I hoped now that we were back at the pack, she'd lessen the smug attitude.

Roman took my hand and led me out of the cabin. I hesitated, because I knew once we left the confines of these walls, I'd have to deal with the reality of my situation. I wasn't sure I was ready for what was to come, but I was also tired of being afraid.

It was time to figure out what the Moon Goddess had meant by her earlier words.

7

ROMAN

Holding Cait, feeling her heart race beneath my touch, was more than I could handle. I'd lost all control, doing exactly what I'd told myself I wouldn't do.

I had wanted to give her time to explain what happened, see how she was physically and mentally, then figure out what might have changed for her while she was gone. Instead, the moment I caught sight of her wolf, all of that went out the window.

My wolf connected with hers, howling inside me with pure, unfiltered bliss. The combination of that and the rage still lingering at having to wait for so long to get to my mate, had me overflowing with emotions I wasn't used to.

All sense fled me until I had Cait alone. Even then, I'd acted on my hormones instead of with my brain. My wolf urged me to claim what was ours. He wanted to show Cait we would never let anything happen to her again.

When she didn't push me away, when I felt the bond between us truly come alive for the first time, I couldn't stop from taking advantage of the moment.

I'd wanted to spend the rest of the night alone with Cait in the cabin, loving her in every way possible, but I hadn't forgotten why we'd been apart in the first place. My mate wouldn't be safe until those who wished her harm no longer walked this earth.

"Do you want to shift and run back together?" I asked Cait.

Her wolf had been stunning. I'd never seen another like her, and while I was intrigued by her new form, I knew the differences were only going to be a bigger problem. Cait would draw unwanted attention.

She nodded. "I wasn't in wolf form for very long before you guys showed up."

"Is it weird having another being inside you?"

Cait's nose scrunched. "She's not very nice. Or at least, she wasn't. She didn't like that I'd, well, uh, chosen to leave."

Her wolf isn't mad anymore. She thought Cait would still fight the bond. They'll find a way to work things out, my own said.

"I'm sure everything will be fine. The more you shift, the quicker you'll connect with the wolf. That should help things," I said, squeezing her hand and taking a step back. "Remember your clothes and picture your wolf."

If Cait appeared naked in front of too many more people, I wasn't sure what I would do. Normally, nudity wasn't a big thing. It happened. But, given she was supposed to be only mine and we hadn't yet "mated," the alpha in me couldn't fathom anyone else enjoying the parts that belonged to me.

She blushed and turned her eyes down. I'd embarrassed her and instantly regretted my selfishness.

I moved back to her, lifting her chin up with my finger. "It's okay, Cait. The rest of us have had our whole lives to figure this out. Nobody expects you to be an expert in shifting right away."

Giving her space once again, I waited for her to transform first in case she needed my help. Also, because I was curious if her shifts would be different from normal wolves.

When I let the change happen, bones broke and elongated or shortened where needed, skin turned to fur, and my predator senses took over, all while colorless magic shimmered around me.

For Cait, that wasn't the case, which a part of me expected, and also hated. It was one more thing that made her stand out.

She closed her eyes, and a purple hue glowed around her skin. Her head tilted forward, and her back arched until a bright light nearly blinded me. She was a dark-violet wolf before I could see anything else.

Her wolf sauntered toward me, head down but eyes on mine. She was strong, yet submissive. Powerful, but I could already tell that power meant nothing to the beast within. She could take it or leave it, and that made her even more glorious than I'd already known.

I bent down onto one knee, greeting the wolf at eye level. Her head pressed against my chest as my hands moved over her front flanks and down her back. "You're more than I deserve," I whispered.

My own wolf hummed inside me, itching to be released but allowing me this moment. We both needed to bond with the new wolf, and I would take every chance I could to do so.

Cait's wolf nipped at my shoulder, nudging me until I nearly fell over. Elation overcame the ire I'd been living in since she'd been taken. I let her take the lead until I knew my wolf couldn't stand the waiting.

She backed up as I stood and shifted.

The new moon had been tonight. My wolf was already amped up from that, but not even the magic from our Moon Goddess could touch what it felt like to be with our mate.

Cait was a few inches shorter than me, and my wolf settled his head over her neck, drawing her in. We stayed close, scenting each other until multiple howls sounded near the pack house. Wolves were returning from the group run that Vaughn had led in my place.

It was time to head back and show them their new female alpha.

Cait matched my stride as we ran toward the pack house. The new moon energized my already invigorated wolf, and I hoped Cait could feel the power of our creator even though it was her first night in her new form.

Other wolves came into view, and my wolf moved ahead of Cait by a few inches. She held her head up high, proud of who she was and more mythical than anything I'd ever seen.

There was an air of confidence about her that I hadn't expected so soon based on her previous reservations to supernaturals, but maybe that was just her wolf taking control.

I believe it's a bit of both, my wolf said, and I had to agree. Though, I wondered how it was for Cait to release control and allow her newly acquired other half to take over. I thought she would be at least slightly agitated, but I wasn't sensing anything of the sort from her.

She had changed irrevocably while she'd been gone, yet I couldn't shake the feeling that her acceptance had come at a significant cost.

Embry was still shifted. Her tan wolf yipped and circled Cait as I gave them some space—something I hadn't been able to do earlier. Cait's seemed hesitant at first, but soon, her flourishing tail swished back and forth, and they pounced on each other.

I shifted back to my human form while they got to know each other, and my parents approached me. "She's stunning, Son," my mother said.

I merely smiled, already fully aware.

"Do you know what happened to her yet?" my dad asked as Cait and Embry trotted toward us.

My head shook. "She wasn't eager to talk about it, and I didn't push yet."

Embry shifted back first; her pink hair was wild and skin glowed from the absorption of the new moon. Cait followed, this time appearing fully clothed, and I breathed a sigh of relief. Over half the pack was present and staring. We'd have to do some explaining soon, but not tonight. Dawn was almost upon us, and the pack would sleep for most of the day.

"I'm sure you all have a lot of questions, but let's stick to normal protocol after a new moon. I will update everyone within the next couple of days with more details. For now, just know Cait is safe, and she has gained her wolf spirit."

Cait moved to my side, taking my hand. I wasn't sure if her wolf had told her to do so, but the gesture made my chest tighten with emotion. She was accepting me in front of our pack, something they hadn't seen yet and I knew would help put them at ease.

"Rest up. We don't know what awaits us, and while I hope it isn't anything I need to concern you all with, we'll need to prepare for the worst-case scenario," I said and waited until most of the gathered pack began to disperse before turning toward Vaughn and my parents.

"Did the run go okay?" I asked my beta.

"Almost as perfect as my Susy. There were a few anxious wolves, but for the most part, it was business as usual." Vaughn grinned widely at me, likely wanting to say more about my and Cait's late arrival, but he thankfully kept his crass words to himself for once.

"Shall we all go catch up in the pack house?" Serene asked with Beatrix at her side.

The witch was fidgety, making me a little nervous, but she'd been away from her coven a lot already. I imagined she was ready to get back to her people and be home for a while.

Cait, my parents, Vaughn, Embry, and I followed the two of them into the pack house. Serene headed into the library and shut the door after we all entered.

Beatrix waved her hands around, sparks of silver magic flickering around her as she muttered to herself. "The room is safe to speak in now. I know you don't want to believe that your pack had anything to do with Cait being taken, but until we have all of the information, we can't be too safe."

This made my wolf furious. He didn't like thinking that wolves we'd give our life for could betray us, but every shifter was also part human. They could all be swayed with the right motivation.

Cait cleared her throat, seeming nervous to speak up. "I don't think anyone in your pack had anything to do with what happened to me."

"Why do you say that?" Embry asked, patting the seat next to her as everyone began to get comfortable in the chairs around the room.

Cait glanced up at me before joining Embry, something akin to fear in her eyes.

"Don't worry. You're here and safe," I said.

She nodded as I stood beside her, then continued. "The witch? Her name is Callista. She came to me as Serene and led me into the forest where you guys found us. I think she was posing as Serene and watching all of us after Kyle's visit."

"How do you know that?" I asked, pushing my ire down, so she could continue. She was about to say something I had hoped wasn't true.

"Because she took me to Cohen's pack. I saw him and Kyle there. Cohen said Kyle had come here to poison Ramona, but because of your reaction around me, he took a chance and gave me the spell instead. I don't know exactly how he did it. Either when he first bumped into me, which wouldn't make sense, or when he kissed the top of my hand as he said goodbye. Whatever Kyle used was made to kill a shifter, but only made me sick. I assume that when they figured out I didn't die, and Callista witnessed what I could do, they made plans to take me."

"What was the point of doing so if they just let you go?" my mother asked.

Cait sighed, pausing before answering the question.

We're going to kill them, my wolf said.

Yes, we are.

"Well, they didn't let me go. Callista thinks she killed me," Cait answered, and I lost all sense of rationale.

My hands transformed into claws, and my teeth turned into sharp canines. I was close to shifting, but a part of me didn't fully let go, in fear of hurting the most precious being in the world to me: my mate.

Cait reached for my forearm, her eyes searing into me. We locked gazes, and I thought that would calm the rage tearing through me, but it didn't.

No, just seeing her concern and fear pushed me over the edge. I hadn't protected Cait, and I'd nearly lost her. How could she even look at me?

A howl ripped from my chest as I took a step back, pacing behind her. I was going to hunt my grandfather and cousin down and destroy whatever plans they had before ending both of their lives, no matter what it took to make that happen.

8

CAIT

I'd known Roman would have an adverse reaction to what had happened to me, but I didn't expect him to wolf out in front of everyone.

At first, I was worried he was going to hurt someone in the room, but when he managed to keep the last sliver of his control in check, my appreciation for him grew by leaps and bounds. Roman was furious on my behalf. He was blitzed out on rage, but strong enough to keep hold on the worst of it. He was a true alpha, and he only had eyes for me.

I didn't know how I had missed the intensity within him before, but I wanted all of it to myself. First, I had to finish telling my story.

Several minutes later, Roman was back to his normal self—at least on the outside—and I continued. I relayed my interactions with the Moon Goddess, including the times she spoke in my head. I explained the moments with Cohen and Kyle and glazed over the ending with Callista.

"You actually throat-punched a bitch? I'm so jealous," Embry said when I finished.

Vaughn shook his head. "Out of all that, *that* was your takeaway?"

She huffed. "No. I also learned I chose well in a bestie. Cait's a badass."

Leave it to the two of them to break some of the tension after my heavy retelling.

Roman's fingers gripped my shoulder as he stood protectively above me. The sun shone into the room from behind us, and exhaustion was setting in for me.

"We'll report their betrayal to the council," Jack said.

Roman snarled. "I don't think so. I'll take care of them myself."

"Son," Jack warned, but Beatrix cut him off.

"There is a reason I came here, a reason I kept you away from Cait as long as I did. Timelines have changed, as I've already mentioned and Cait has, too. While you're feeling murderous, you'll need to take those aggressions out on a different foe before you're able to face Cohen."

This had my attention.

"Why should I listen to you?" Roman snapped.

"Because if you don't, Sam won't be making it back home."

The connection I felt to Roman flared to life as he held painfully tight to me. My hand covered his, hoping to ease some of his rage.

"Where is Sam?" Roman asked with an eerie calm.

"She's stuck in Australia. Sort of," the witch replied.

"What do you mean 'sort of'?" Vaughn asked.

Beatrix stood, streams of magic bouncing between her hands. I was transfixed by them until she clapped her hands, making me jump in my seat.

When she pulled her hands apart again, an image appeared of a boulder on an empty beach with waves just a few yards away. It was massive in size, and there appeared to be screaming faces carved into the hard surface.

"This is dark magic. The rock is a host witches use to trap souls while they inhabit the bodies of their victims. At least, that is the typical use of this particular stone. These are powerful witches who have died and been brought back to life. The kind that those of us who know better kill at every chance we get."

Just when I had thought I was getting the hang of this supernatural life, Beatrix had to throw the biggest of bombshells on us.

"Are you saying a *witch* is inhabiting the body of *my* cousin?" Roman asked very slowly, words dripping with malice that made my skin crawl. He'd certainly had a rough day, and every ounce of alpha power was pouring from him, making me squirm in my seat.

Our mate is strong. He will protect us, my wolf said.

She wasn't saying anything I didn't already know, but Roman had always been so calm, cool, and collected before. From the moment they found me, I'd been seeing a different side to him, one that felt more real than anything before.

Not that I didn't believe he wasn't as caring as he'd been previously, but the Roman before me was raw and raging, and I was intrigued.

We will fight with him, my wolf added.

Hmmm, I wasn't sure how that would work. There was a lot I still had to figure out about me, or at least me and my wolf. She was being nicer, but I wasn't convinced that would last forever. I still needed to decide how to approach her attitude.

I'd missed the first part of Beatrix's response, but tuned back in at the right time to get the gist of what was going on.

"Sam was ill-informed about her mission. She'd unexpectedly had help, but it wasn't enough against the dark witches. Like I said before, they'll use the stone to store souls while they inhabit the body, but sometimes it's used to offer up their sacrifices in exchange for continuing to draw the dark powers of the stone."

"Are you saying Sam is being used as a sacrifice?" Jack asked when shock prevented the rest of us from speaking.

Beatrix nodded. "If she doesn't get out in time, yes. Her body will be absorbed by the magic of the rock, and the physical part of your niece will be turned to dust. Sam killed several of the witches on her own, as did the help she had, but I don't know what happened to him. That wasn't part of the business I was asked to pass along."

"So, how can we get her back?" Vaughn asked.

"That I can't help you with. I need to get back to my coven. We have our own messes to deal with in California, but I promised my ancestors I'd set you on the right path. As long as you're not too bullheaded, then I believe I've done that."

Roman paced as Embry reached for me and asked, "What about Cait?"

"I was wrong before. Cait is a wolf shifter, even though she is different. The Moon Goddess made her creation just as intended, and I can only make assumptions on anything more than that, which won't be very helpful. I'm sure the rest of you will figure it out," Beatrix answered and stood.

Roman's head snapped up, eyes filled with fury. "You're just going to drop all of this on us and leave without a solution to the problem? Like this doesn't involve your kind as well?"

If I didn't know Roman, I'd have cowered down. The rage dripping from his words broke my heart.

"They might be witches, but they're not *my* kind. I don't have a magical solution for you, but I have some advice. Use your alpha power. You can control your wolves. Make Sam come back to you," Beatrix replied as she proceeded to the door, but looked back at the last second. "I'll leave portal spells with Serene to help you get there and back faster."

I thought for a moment Roman was going to stop her, but he said nothing more as Serene and Roman's parents followed the witch out and it was just me, Roman, Embry, and Vaughn left in the room.

"Well, isn't this just like a bitch's bad tit?" Vaughn said, and I snorted.

"I think your parents dropped you on your head a time or two when you were little," I said, glad he'd broken some of the tension in the room.

Roman turned toward the three of us. "We need to leave." Then, he glanced at me, and his darkening eyes told me where his true fear lay. He knew I wasn't ready to fight witches, and he didn't want to leave me, but his love for his cousin was too big to do nothing when there was a chance she could die.

I reached for him, offering any sort of comfort I could. What he'd done for me, stealing me away and showing me how much he still cared in the cabin? It had been just what I needed. Hopefully, my small actions told him how much things had changed for me while I'd been gone.

My touch broke the rigidness of Roman's stance as Vaughn spoke.

"We can handle this. Sam had been set up, it sounds like. We just need a quick in-and-out plan. It shouldn't take much to call her out from the rock, if that will work. If it doesn't, then we leave and re-evaluate," the beta said.

Roman's stare bored into me. His worries were so strong, they felt tangible. "I can't leave you."

"I can stay here with your parents. It's not that big of a deal. I won't leave the pack," I said.

"You didn't intend to leave the pack last time, either. It's my job to protect you, and I won't fail again," he replied with little emotion, but I could tell his flat tone was hiding a hell of a lot of rage.

"What if we wait just a day? Cait was making a lot of progress before things went to shit. Now that she's full wolf, it could be worth taking the time to see. If things go well, she might even save the day," Embry said.

Roman whipped his hardened stare toward my best friend and took a step toward her, but I moved between them. "Listen to me very carefully. I realize I am completely out of my element here, but Embry has a point. I would never force you to bring me, but if I can help, then it's worth finding out, right? If you try to keep me 'protected', I'm going to continue to be a liability. We need to figure out what I'm capable of," I said, keeping my head high while meeting his gaze.

His cheek twitched, but he didn't respond. Good, he was at least seeing reason. I hoped he understood that I wasn't a princess to be kept in a tower for all eternity.

We have more magic within us than any wolf shifter in this pack. We could lead them if we wanted, my wolf said.

Yeah, well, I'm assuming that power comes directly from you, and if we can't learn to work together, then it won't mean shit to anyone, I replied.

She was silent a few beats before replying. *I was angry with your stupidity. As long as you're not stupid, we should be just fine.*

I rolled my eyes. *She* was going to take a lot of getting used to.

"I'm sorry, Ro, but I agree with Embry. I can catch Beatrix before she leaves and see if there was a specific timeframe to make sure Sam will be okay with one more day," Vaughn said.

Roman's chest rumbled as his fingers stretched and curled at his side. His lack of response told me that the alpha in him knew we'd all made good points, but the mate in him was not okay with the situation being shoved into his face.

Embry grabbed my hand. "I realize you haven't slept, but is now too soon? Then, we can take naps this afternoon, have another session in the evening and get a good night's rest before we leave tomorrow morning."

I can provide you with enough energy. Let's show them what we're capable of, my wolf said in a tone too confident for my liking.

Given Roman hadn't shot the idea down immediately, I took the opening while I could. "My wolf says we're ready, so let's go."

Before I even finished my sentence, Embry was pulling me to the door, but stopped suddenly, causing me to crash into her back.

Embry's head lowered and she stayed facing the wall. I turned back to Roman who was stalking toward me.

"We need to talk about this," he said.

"We just did. I'm not saying it's a done deal. If Beatrix says Sam needs you now, or if I can't prove I'm capable of helping, then I'll stay locked up inside the pack house for however long you're gone." If I was being honest, some alone time and rest sounded like a dream, but more than that, I wanted to help.

He nodded. "Fine, but no more than two hours of training right now. I don't want anything to happen because you were pushed too hard, too soon."

Embry made a strangled noise from behind me, and I'd forgotten he'd used his alpha juju on my best friend. Not okay.

I shoved a finger in his chest. "Stop being an…alpha. Embry is off limits to you as of this moment."

His eyes widened and lips twitched, the first sign of anything positive since we entered the library. "Are you telling me what to do with my wolves?" he challenged.

"No. Just this one. At least for now."

He leaned down, kissing my forehead and sending heat straight through my body. "Very well, *Mate*. Whatever you say. Let's go see what kind of abilities you've been gifted with."

I shook my head. He was giving me an emotional overload, and I wouldn't be able to concentrate as well with him watching.

"That's a no as well. You have things to do here with Vaughn, I'm sure." I glanced at the beta, but the chicken shit was looking everywhere but at us. "Do whatever it is alphas are supposed to do before they leave town. I'll come find you when we're done."

His hands wrapped around my upper arms, pulling

me close. "So, we can take the nap together that Embry mentioned you'd need?"

My face must have turned ten shades of red, because Roman smirked right before pressing his lips to mine. Then, he whispered, "Pushing me in front of my wolves is cause for punishment. You might not be ready for it yet, but I will remember each and every time you publicly put me in my place."

Roman turned me back toward Embry, gave my ass a smack, and gently shoved me toward the door.

Holy shit, I couldn't breathe and really wished our nap time was right freaking then. On the positive side, Roman wasn't raging like he'd been just a few minutes before.

Embry managed to hold her snickers in until we opened the front door of the house, but once they started, she turned into a damn hyena with her laughter.

"You shouldn't be laughing at me. I was standing up for you!" I shout-hissed at her as we crossed the yard.

Embry's giggles turned into sobs within seconds. She paused in the grass and threw her arms around me. "I thought I'd lost you."

Embry had never cried with me before. Never been sad or overly upset. Her sudden onset of emotions threw my own into overdrive and, before I knew it, we were bawling all over each other.

I'd done my best to pretend I hadn't died and come back to life. The truth was that this new world I'd found myself in was not for the faint of heart, and I needed to make sure dying wasn't on my agenda for many, many decades. Well, at least not again.

"It's okay, Em. I'm here, and I'm okay, and you're going to help make sure nobody can ever kidnap me again," I said as I wiped tears from my cheeks.

She backed up and, even with glossy eyes, smirked at me. "Unless it's Roman. He seems to be really fond of that."

I knew she was going to want to know what happened at the cabin earlier, but I wasn't up for kissing and telling. Not then anyway.

You shouldn't ever be. What happens between you and our mate is sacred, my wolf said with disgust I assumed was toward me.

Listen here, Wolfette. I'm about damn tired of your attitude. I didn't ask for this any more than you did, but I'm doing my best. Yes, I made some mistakes, but cut me some damn slack. I didn't know about this world until a few weeks ago. You've been around how many lifetimes?

Okay, I'd definitely meant to have this conversation in a more adult way, but her brashness was too much.

She was quiet, and Embry was staring at me like I was crazy, but I wasn't moving until the wolf spoke.

This is my fifth lifetime. I've lived for nearly seven hundred years.

Her voice was calm and sad and jaded. A pile of guilt slammed into me as I realized she'd been alone, without her other half, for a very long time. She was born in a time much different from mine, and we both needed to find a way to compromise.

I'm sorry for snapping. We just need more time to get to know each other. Can we start with what you're capable of? I assume most of my skills will come from you?

She huffed. *All of them will.*

And back to the smug wolf. This was going to be interesting.

Then, she gave me whiplash as she spoke again. *I'm sorry, too. You were growing in power on your own before Luna had to take your magic away. I'm sure you will find your own abilities as well.*

My jaw dropped ever so slightly. I hadn't expected an apology, and I didn't want to make a big deal out of it, so I said my thanks and carried on with Embry.

"Uh, want to tell me what that was about?" she asked.

I shrugged. "My wolf and I are getting to know each other."

"I can't even imagine how hard that is, but you have no idea how grateful I am that you are like me. You are my person—the only one who has ever accepted me for who I was—and you have no idea how sad it made me these few years to keep who I really am a secret from you."

I looped my arm through hers. "It all worked out the way it was supposed to, or close to it, I guess. I don't like that everything is so rushed. I really would have preferred the slow and steady plans the Moon Goddess had for me before."

"Don't worry, Cait. We're going to turn you into the second-most badass wolf there ever was."

My brow raised. "Second-most?"

"Obviously, I'm not going to let you show me up." She winked and sprinted away from me, calling back over her shoulder. "Training starts now. Last one to the field does dishes for a month!"

She was ridiculous, but I loved her anyway and raced after. There was no way I would be doing dishes for that long.

9

CAIT

Unfortunately for the competitive side in both of us, we tied. I'd considered it a win for me since she had a head start, but Embry wouldn't hear anything I had to say. She was just pouty because she hadn't left my ass in the dust.

The faster my legs moved, the stronger I felt. Every part of me pricked with energy that was begging to be let free. Instincts screamed at me to shift or run or… anything active, but I trusted Embry and wanted to see what she had planned for me.

You have a natural talent to protect yourself. You don't need to be wasting your time with this, my wolf said. This time it was without malice; she was just stating a fact.

Well, I want to be sure I don't get anyone else killed because I didn't try to prepare myself. So, unless you want to begin showing me some things, let Embry help.

Just as I finished speaking, my best friend, the person I trusted most in the world, pounced on me without notice. My hands went up to defend myself, and sparks of purple pricked along my exposed skin.

Embry hissed as she made contact but kept coming at me. She swung a nasty right hook, slamming into my jaw. I stumbled back, but only for a moment before I lunged at her. My feet moved with effortless speed. My eyes caught sight of every speck in the air. My muscles coiled and then sprung to life as we connected.

My left arm wrapped around Embry's neck, bringing her to the ground as I secured my legs around her. She was on top of me, but I had all of the power.

"That wasn't very nice," I hissed.

"You weren't paying attention. Lesson one: always have one eye on your surroundings," she muttered beneath my hold.

I released her with a solid shove and stood up. She was grinning widely. "What's the smile for?"

"We don't need to do this. You're going to be just fine. Regardless, we can have some fun and make Roman feel better all at the same time."

"What happened to you the day Callista showed up?" I asked since it hadn't come up during the earlier conversations.

Embry's shoulders stiffened and her eyes hardened. "That bitch had been posing as Serene all day. She'd told me there was a wolf pup stuck up a tree and she was too old to get him down. It seemed like something she would say, so I followed her about ten feet into the woods. When I questioned why I couldn't hear the pup, she hit me in the head with magic that knocked my ass out cold. Something I plan to pay back as soon as we find her."

"I think she has a lot of payback coming her way when we go to West Texas," I said, knowing I'd love to kick her ass again. Even more so, a part of me would prefer to rip her to shreds, but killing… That didn't seem like something I was capable of.

Preemptive killing isn't something any good wolf should be capable of, but when it comes down to your life or that of those you care about, sometimes it's the only option, my wolf said, and her words slammed into me with a realization I wasn't quite ready for.

"Have you killed anyone?" I asked Embry.

She nodded. "Just once. A rogue wolf who thought he could have whatever he wanted. I showed him he couldn't. It's not common practice for us to do the killing. A lot of the time, the wolf or supernatural council will get involved before things escalate far enough that heads start flying."

"Why aren't they involved now?" I asked, considering I'd been kidnapped.

"Roman would have reached out to them if Beatrix hadn't shown up when she did. He was making his way home, even if he hadn't realized it, before we even called him back. Jack and Ramona would have pushed him for that route as well."

"Why not involve the wolf council now?" I asked, still not understanding how their help wouldn't be welcome.

Embry sighed. "This has grown too big. Our own

council would pass along our request and, frankly, I'm not sure how trustworthy any of them are. With everything changing, we have to be careful who we trust for now. If there comes a point when we've gotten in too far over our heads, then we can send a call out to the councils."

"What about your parents? Can't you reach out to them?" I remembered Embry telling me that they worked for the Supernatural Council and she rarely saw them.

She shook her head. "It doesn't work like that. Even if I could get a hold of them, if I say one word about what's going on here, they'll be required to tell their superiors."

"How does that work for Sam then? She knows about me, right?"

"Sam contracts for the council. She did things the smart way for those in her line of work. She isn't stuck under the council's thumb the same way as my parents."

I rubbed my hand over the back of my neck. There were a lot of moving parts to this world, and I worried it was going to take me too long to figure it all out.

How about less talking and more fighting? I'd like to meet Embry's wolf in a more official setting than before. If we're to be around them all the time, it will be good to set the hierarchy, my wolf said.

Hierarchy? We're not in the 1500s, and this isn't a kingdom.

You're right, but we are in a wolf pack and that is how

things are done. There will be times when you are challenged and need to put another in their place in order to keep yours. You need to remember that, or the wolves will never respect you as the alpha's mate.

Son of a bitch, she had a point.

Fine, but don't hurt Embry's wolf. She would never challenge us.

I'll be the judge of that.

"Chatty wolf this morning?" Embry asked teasingly.

"Just filling me in on all things wolf etiquette. She'd like us to shift."

"We can train as wolves, but just remember, you can't always change to your wolf to protect yourself. You need to know how to handle difficult situations in both forms, using all of your strengths and wit."

I nodded, understanding that if someone was to grab me and people not supernatural were around, I couldn't let them see what I'd become. Some might be ready for the paranormal to make their appearance, but I had a feeling most of the world would be how I was and let fear rule their actions.

Thankfully, I'd died and moved past that. Funny. Not funny.

My wolf pushed at me, wanting to take charge. I didn't fight her on purpose, but I worried the shift was going to hurt. I'd been running on adrenaline and new life before. This time, it was just me and her and we were completely safe.

Don't focus on the pain and there won't be any, she said,

and I rolled my eyes, thinking there was no way it could be that easy.

Still, I took her advice and thought about my too-tight yoga pants and tank top I was still wearing, wondering what had happened to my other clothes when I transformed and forgot about them. Did they get shredded to pieces? Did they disappear into the unknown? These were serious questions that needed serious answers.

Good job. You successfully distracted yourself with stupidity, my wolf droned, and I realized we had already changed.

I hadn't felt a thing. Maybe it was different for a wolf like mine. She was a solid form, but there was a glow about her that the others didn't have. Not to mention, the purple color that stood out like a sore thumb.

The coloring is your fault. I was a deep umber in my last life and absolutely perfect, she added.

Huh. The violet-to-black colors must have come from the magic within the mark, then. Either way, we still stood out. That was going to be an issue at some point, I was sure of it.

Embry was still human and staring in awe at us. She circled around, her hand out cautiously. My wolf nudged her, giving the permission Embry seemed to be seeking.

"Your coat is so soft and long. Almost fluffy, but more like its lighter than air. It's incredible." Embry's fingers scratched down my wolf's spine, and we instantly relaxed. Apparently, this was a weak spot for my wolf.

"Can I braid your tail?" Embry asked, and my wolf's head whipped around, baring teeth. "Got it. No braiding."

Embry backed up and finally shifted. Her desert-tan wolf was about the same height and girth as mine. Her paws and the tip of her tail changed to a deep brown, and her eyes were still the same bright blue, filled with mischief.

Can we talk to them? I asked my wolf.

No, we aren't officially a part of the pack yet. Wolves don't communicate with others unless they share a bond.

Do I have to be fully mated to Roman to be part of the pack?

My wolf sighed. *No, they are two separate processes.*

Why did it seem like you were talking with Roman's wolf when he first showed up? I asked.

Mates don't need words to tell the other how they feel.

I had a feeling I was going to be learning multiple new things, every day, for the rest of my new life.

Embry circled us, and my wolf stayed put with her head high. She didn't seem at all worried about the glint in Embry's eyes, one I knew meant she was up to something.

I tried to force my wolf to move, but she had all of the control and I didn't know how to take it from her, something I planned to figure out very soon.

Embry lowered herself to the ground, readying for her attack.

Aren't you going to do something? I asked.

I am. The first thing to remember about your opponent is that they almost always believe they have the upper hand right until the point that they don't.

Embry swiped a paw at us, missing by mere inches. Power swirled from inside my wolf that I could still feel myself, as if I was in my human form. I stopped trying to control her and, instead, used my senses to learn. While my wolf might be smug as hell, she was old and powerful. I'd be an idiot to ignore what she was trying to teach me in her own way.

Just as Embry's wolf finally made her move, energy blossomed from within my own and expelled from our form. Purple swirls appeared, just like when I'd been meditating with Embry in this same field. The power knocked Embry back several yards and created a cocoon around us.

Was that you or me? I asked.

It was both of us.

Embry wasn't one to back down, and she stupidly charged forward again.

Can this hurt her?

Only if I want it to, but don't worry, the only thing hurt will be her pride, my wolf answered, and I was actually okay with this. I loved Embry, but this could be fun.

Let's show her what we can do, then, I said and worked with my wolf to move as one. I wasn't sure how this wolf-human thing was supposed to work, but something told me that eventually, we should work as one mind, one being.

With personality differences aside, this was the first step toward making that happen.

We feigned to our left, drawing Embry closer, then leaped over, swiping at her back with a paw before nipping at her front quarters.

Embry snarled at the unexpected moves, getting in a solid kick to our gut with her back leg. In response, we leaped into the air, landing on top of my best friend and grabbing hold of her neck.

Our wolves snarled at each other as my energy grew. I pushed on the sensations until they physically left my body. Violet whisps moved around us as Embry's wolf stopped struggling beneath us. When we backed off, she stayed on the ground, unmoving.

What did we do? I shrieked at my wolf.

She's just taking a little nap.

I nudged Embry's wolf with our snout, rolling her a couple of inches. She flinched but didn't wake.

She is a worthy companion. I accept her wolf.

I chuckled. *I'm not so sure she'll accept you after this.*

Yes, she will. Like I said, she's worthy.

As Embry's wolf finally began to stand, I shifted back to human form—with my clothes intact. My hair was still a hot mess and was going to need lots of conditioner when we were done here, but otherwise, I was feeling better than ever.

If I really thought about my situation, my mental state might not be faring so well, but I'd made a choice when I'd been stuck underground. I wasn't going to live in fear anymore, and if that meant ignoring some of the things that life threw my way, then so be it.

"Holy shit, Cait. What the hell was that?" Embry asked as she joined me.

"No idea, but it was kind of fun, huh?" I grinned.

Her hand slapped down on my shoulder. "Yes, it was, but you ever tell anyone that happened, and I'll unfriend you."

"I'm pretty sure unfriending me isn't an option at this point."

She scoffed. "Either way, I'll figure out how to get back at you if you tell a soul."

For the rest of the not-really-training, we stayed in human form. Embry taught me a lot, but I was also able to do more than I would have ever expected without needing guidance. This made me confident about going back to Roman and telling him I was ready.

Even more than that, I was eager for a hot shower, my own clothes, copious amounts of food, and sleep. All in that order.

What about our mate? my wolf asked, and her desire to be close to him made my stomach ache and pulse quicken.

Don't worry, Wolfette. We'll see our mate soon enough.

10

CAIT

The stank I washed off myself was beyond words. Mortification filled me at the thought of Roman having endured that smell while his hand was shoved down my pants and his face all over my upper half earlier.

He is our mate. We don't ever need to be ashamed of our presence around him, my wolf said, but I ignored her and continued with my shower.

I had no idea how long I'd been in the bathroom, but I also didn't care. I'd been kidnapped, kept underground, had the shit beaten out of me, died, and came back to life. All of that combined meant I deserved more than a little "me" time.

That was only until I heard Roman's voice in the living room of Embry's house. I was naked and wet, and he was just on the other side of the door. If Embry hadn't been around, there was a decent chance I'd invite him in, but she was, so I didn't.

If she's really your friend, she'd understand we have needs, my wolf said.

Are you making my libido go crazy around him? Because I sure as hell didn't want to hump him like this before.

It's in our nature. I'm not doing anything that isn't natural to who we are.

Smug. Wolf.

Now that my relaxation had been taken away, I finished rinsing off and was glad I'd brought fresh clothes into the bathroom with me. I wasn't sure Roman —or I—would have survived a naked me walking down the hallway.

I braided my hair after brushing it to save time, then exited the bathroom. Roman's shoulders relaxed, and his eyes bored into me as soon as I appeared.

"How are you doing?" he asked, glancing over my body and giving me a visual inspection that didn't help my overall wellbeing.

"Great now that I'm clean. I'll be even better after I eat, then sleep," I answered honestly.

"I brought you some food. I thought maybe we could eat together. Embry had to go run an errand," he said.

"She 'had' to, or it was highly encouraged that she do so by her alpha?" I teased.

He shrugged. "Maybe a little of both."

My cheeks heated as we stared at each other. I was never going to survive these new hormones. They would be the end of me.

They wouldn't be so severe if you mated him. It's going to happen eventually. Why do you torture yourself waiting? my wolf asked, and I genuinely believed she was confused as to why I hadn't jumped Roman the moment I saw him.

Because that's not how things are done. People date, sometimes even get married first before having sex. I've only known him a few weeks.

That's what people in your old life do. Not ones in this new life.

Her answer was honest and accurate, but it didn't change my mind. I'd only had sex with two people in my past. My still very human-thinking mind had a hard time with just jumping into bed with Roman. Now, the things we'd done earlier… Those types of things weren't out of the question while we got to know each other better.

Roman cleared his throat and moved to the kitchen. He had food laid out including sandwiches, veggies, fried chicken, and chocolate-covered strawberries.

I nearly began drooling I was so starving. "Strawberries are my favorite."

He picked one up and held it toward me. "Then, you should have that first."

I reached for the deliciousness, but he moved it out of my reach before returning to feed me himself.

Yep. Death was coming for me.

My lips parted ever so slowly as my chest rose and fell quicker by the second. Biting down, I moaned as the chocolatey goodness melted against my tongue.

"This is so good," I murmured.

Roman's other hand brushed a strand of my hair away as his thumb stroked my cheek. "What else do you want?"

Damn, that was a loaded question, and the bastard knew it, but I managed to shove my hormones down—barely—and turned toward the rest of the food. I put a sandwich and some veggies on a plate before taking a seat.

He grinned while getting his own food and sat next to me, his leg resting against mine and the heat from his skin branding my own.

My food was devoured in mere minutes, and I went for seconds, this time grabbing the fried chicken and two more strawberries.

Roman eyed the dessert and smirked at me as he finished his food. "Beatrix said we need to leave tonight instead of tomorrow morning. You'll want to make sure you rest after we're done eating," he said.

"That was my plan," I replied, wondering if he had hoped for a different response.

"Do you mind if I stay and lay with you?"

I laughed. I couldn't help myself. It wasn't like he didn't already sense the sexual tension between us. "Are we actually going to sleep?"

He nodded, and there was a happiness shining through his eyes I wasn't used to. "Yes, Cait. I promise to always put your needs first, and you need to rest before we leave. Embry said you did well, and she has no concerns about you going to Australia with us.

While shifters don't need as much sleep as humans, we do still require it to be at our best."

"Then, I don't mind if you stay." To be honest, I'd probably sleep better. I had been slightly worried that visions of my time with Callista would keep me from truly resting, and not being alone would hopefully help with that.

We finished our food, and I led the way back to my room. Suddenly, everything seemed too small to fit us both, but I ignored my nerves and lay on top of the covers. It was early afternoon, and the house was warm from the heat outside. No need for blankets.

Roman followed my actions and lifted my head so he could wrap his arm around me. I gladly snuggled into his chest, sighing at how perfect it felt to be in his arms. Wolfette was right. I was fighting the inevitable, but Rome wasn't built in a day, and I couldn't change all of me that quickly, either.

He stroked my back, holding me close. My breathing evened, and I sighed, content and safe. Everything was going to be okay. I was alive. I was a wolf shifter. I had my best friend around, and I'd found the person created specifically for me in this world.

Now, we just needed to get his cousin back in one piece and we'd be another step closer to finding a new normal.

Though, given what I was, I wasn't sure normal was the right word for the life I'd suddenly found myself permanently tied to.

11

ROMAN

I couldn't remember the last time I'd slept. Even before Cait had been taken, any rest had been sparse, but as I held her in my arms, listening to the calming breaths she took while laying on my chest, I finally felt as if I could take this moment to myself.

My hold on her tightened as much as I thought I could get away with without waking her up. Her hand held firmly to my waist, and I wondered if she even knew she was doing it while she slept.

Even though Cait seemed to be much more accepting since we'd found her, there was still a hesitation I could sense during our interactions, one that I thought I would hate, but instead, I admired. If she'd done a complete one-eighty on me, I might have been more worried. There were many things I'd learned to appreciate about my mate. Her stubbornness was one of them.

Cait was a challenge for me, and there was nothing I

wanted more than to overcome any obstacles she threw my way. As long as I could have her like this, I'd wait forever for her to be ready for anything more.

Her wolf is spectacular, my own said.

She is, but that's also something we'll need to worry about, I replied.

Something tells me that while our mate will draw attention wherever she goes, most will be smart enough to leave her be.

And what about those not smart enough?

We'll be there to strike them down where they stand if they dare to touch what is ours. I could hear the pride in my wolf's voice.

He wasn't wrong, either. No matter what happened, no matter who came for us, there was nothing that would keep me from Cait so long as she wanted me by her side.

With that thought, I finally let myself sleep, knowing that getting Sam back wasn't going to be an easy feat.

///

THE SWEET SCENT OF CAIT WOKE ME UP, AND AS I OPENED my eyes, I caught hers staring at me. Instead of being embarrassed at having been caught, she grinned. "You talk in your sleep."

"I do not," I replied sharply.

She nodded. "I beg to differ, but I'll let you believe what you want."

"What did I say?" I asked, hoping I hadn't made myself look like an idiot.

"I think I'll keep that to myself given you seem to believe you don't sleep-talk."

I grabbed on to Cait's waist, moving her so she was flush against me. "There aren't secrets between mates," I growled.

Her cheeks flushed, and I realized my mistake too late. I didn't want to push her into anything she wasn't ready for. I'd already gone too far at my cabin, but it was instinctual for me to hold her this way. Anything less was going to be harder than I was prepared for.

She recovered well enough to lean forward and shock the hell out of me by kissing me first. "It isn't a secret. We're both well aware of what you said, but I'll keep the details to myself."

Cait seemed pleased with herself as she crawled off of me, so I let her have her fun. Something told me if I pushed her any further, it would only be more torturous for me anyway.

"It's nearly eight P.M. What time are we leaving, and how are we getting to Australia?" Cait asked as she undid the braid in her hair.

I stood and stretched, not missing the way she watched as I moved. "Beatrix followed through and left us with the spells to create temporary portals. Handy things to have. That's how I'd gotten from here to Fae Islands and to Australia. Except, I'd only brought two with me and had to fly home after finding you."

Her eyes widened. "Were you on my flight?"

"Yep. Embry had booked you the last first-class seat, and I'd been stuck at the back of the plane, tortured by your scent wafting toward me the entire time."

"Why didn't Vaughn pick you up, too?" she asked.

"Because I hadn't told anyone I was coming back early. I needed some time to sort through my thoughts. Little did I know, my distraction would be waiting in the driveway for me."

She shied away. "You'd been so angry with me."

I stepped to her, turning her toward me and holding her close until she looked up. "I was never angry with *you*. I was upset with the situation, not knowing what you were and the danger it posed. Being an alpha's mate comes with its own challenges under normal circumstances, and there wasn't anything normal about you." I kissed her forehead. "Now, I wouldn't have it any other way."

Cait relaxed within my grasp, and I pulled her in until her head rested against my chest. We stood this way for several minutes until she leaned back. "You never said what time we were supposed to leave."

"I'd like to leave within the hour. I need to go finalize things with Vaughn. Do you want to come with me or stay here? Embry is back and in her room," I said.

Her face scrunched. "How do you know that?"

"Alpha perks. When we get home, we'll make you part of the pack, and you'll get some of the extra senses, like speaking telepathically. Later, if we bond, you'll also take on some of my alpha abilities." Gods, I hated saying the word "if", but I refused to force her into something she didn't want wholeheartedly. However, I wanted to make sure the idea of us bonding wasn't too far from her mind.

When Cait grabbed my hand, her own shook, telling me she was nervous, but she pushed through anyway. "It's not if, but when, Roman. I just need time, but I want that time to be spent with you if that makes sense."

Unfortunately, it did make sense. She grew up in a world different from mine. I respected Cait, and that meant I accepted all of who she was, including the parts that were bound to drive me crazy.

"It's okay, Cait. I understand. Let's just take one thing at a time. We'll get Sam home and then celebrate you joining the pack. After that, I'll hold Cohen, Kyle, and Callista responsible for what they did to you."

The ire I'd nearly exploded with before tried taking hold again, but I shoved it down. Letting my emotions guide me wasn't going to fix anything, and I needed to keep that at the forefront of my mind.

That didn't mean I'd take things easy on those who played a hand in taking my mate. I'd hopefully be taking care of that issue right after we returned, but I'd also make sure things were done right. I wouldn't let my actions take me away from Cait. Not ever.

Cait didn't respond to my comment about her captors and didn't seem eager to join me, so I kissed her goodbye. "I'll be back soon, and the three of us will head out."

"Won't we need more people than that?" Cait asked with surprise.

"Too many will draw attention. My hope is Beatrix was right and I'll be able to command Sam out of the magical hold from the stone."

She nodded, and then I kissed her once more, saying our goodbyes. I headed toward the pack house to find Vaughn and make sure he had everything handled before I left. I'd been gone too much lately, but hopefully the pack understood it was only to make things better around here.

An alpha with his true mate was the strongest of our kind. Cait would only fortify my ability to keep them safe. We just needed to get through a few more obstacles to make that happen.

Vaughn was waiting for me on the front steps. "Alpha."

"Beta. Anything to report?" I asked.

"Pack members want to know when you plan to give them more information about what happened to Cait. They want to know if trouble is coming our way. I didn't tell them about Sam, but I did say you were working on something important and might not be able to address things as soon as you had hoped."

Shit, I'd forgotten that I promised to inform them of the current happenings. "Thank you. I'll send out an email to hold them over. Word will travel fast enough for those not online."

Most of our older generation refused to use the new technology, preferring information come in a more personal way. I didn't disagree with them, but sometimes, things needed to be done as efficiently as possible.

"Are you prepared for the witches you might have to contend with?" Vaughn asked.

"I'm not worried about them, as long as it's not a whole coven. If we're in over our heads, we'll come back to form a new plan, but we both know the longer Sam is stuck in that stone, the more likely we are to lose her. I won't leave her to that fate if I can help it."

Vaughn's fist connected with the porch railing. "Are you sure I can't go with you?"

"Given everything happening with Cohen, I need you here. I can't leave the pack for my parents to handle when we don't know exactly what he's up to."

Vaughn knew this already, but I also knew why he'd asked again about coming with us. Sam meant a lot to more than just me. She was a valued member in our pack and like family to Vaughn as well.

"Do you need anything before you go?" he asked.

"Just the spells from Beatrix and my dagger." I didn't often use weapons on missions, but I couldn't be too careful with this one. Bringing Cait felt right, but that didn't mean a small part of me wasn't worried I was making the biggest mistake of my life.

If anything happened to her because I didn't force her to stay with the pack, I would never forgive myself.

Everything had to go perfectly. Anything less was unacceptable.

12

CAIT

As soon as I entered the living room, Embry jumped down from her loft and scared the hell out of me. "Good evening, roomie. Have a nice *nap*?" she asked with a grin.

"Yes, we napped. Fully clothed, on top of the covers." Like I would have had sex in the same house as her with her wolf ears. Not my kind of kink.

"Unfortunately, I believe you. You'll break sooner or later. I can smell it on you," she said, and my jaw nearly came unhinged.

"That's…not cool. Why am I not getting all these extra senses? I mean I'm happy to not smell whatever… Never mind. I can't have this conversation right now. We have to get ready to find Sam."

I needed to figure out all this wolf stuff sooner rather than later. It was going to get really freaking awkward as I spent more time around Roman.

"Oh, calm down. It's normal for wolves to smell all

sorts of emotions. Most of the time, we ignore them, but since you're my best friend, I have a vested interest." She grinned, but I didn't feel any better.

"As for why you're not sensing these things, I assume it's because you're on overload. Too many things happening for you to slow down your mind enough to search. I've been doing this my whole life. Don't set yourself up for disappointment by thinking you'll be an expert wolf overnight."

She was right. Even Roman had said something similar earlier, but given that the fighting had come natural to me, I assumed the rest would as well. That was what I got for assuming.

"Do you have dark pants and a shirt you won't mind getting bloodied if needed?" Embry asked.

"Yes to the shirt, but no to the pants. I only have blue jeans or shorts. Why?"

"Because if we need to hide, darker colors are always better. Let me grab something for you." Embry took a few steps back to her loft stairs and was up them before I could blink. Again, I really needed to zero in on these new talents. Her agility skills were new life goals.

Before I knew it, two pairs of pants were thrown down at me, one of them black jeans and the other leather. I raised a brow at her from where she stood above me. "Leather, really?"

She shrugged. "You'll look hot, and it would make things more interesting."

"You're a terrible friend."

"But you love me anyway," she called out as she disappeared back into her room.

I tossed the leather pants down on the coffee table. I didn't need to look hot for my first outing or mission or whatever this was. I needed to be comfortable and capable.

Going back into my room, I changed into the pants and grabbed a charcoal-grey tank top from the closet. It was one I wouldn't be sad about ruining if things got crazy. Next, I slipped into my favorite black converse, again going for comfort instead of style. I hadn't worn them since arriving in Texas since it was so damn hot all the time.

Lastly, I went to the bathroom, brushed my hair again, and put it in another braid since the previous one had been ruined during my nap. I took a look in the mirror. My green eyes were brighter than they'd ever been before, and with the tiniest specks of purple in them. I liked purple and all, but if my hair started changing colors, too, I was going to have a problem.

Embry was waiting for me when I came out. She was wearing a very similar outfit, and her hair was also braided. She gave me a nod of approval before we headed out the door toward the pack house. When we arrived, I followed her to the stairs that led to Roman's office. He was in there with his dad and Vaughn.

They all seemed more worried than I liked, but when Roman laid eyes on me, some of his tension disappeared.

"What's the plan, boss?" Embry asked, taking a seat in front of Roman's desk.

I stood awkwardly, unsure if I should stick closer to Embry or go to Roman's side. I knew which was better, but it seemed like too much.

Don't let your emotions cloud your instincts. Especially not with Roman and not when you're on a mission, my wolf offered as advice.

She was right, on both accounts—the former seeming to be the easier of the two. Nobody in the room would blink an eye at seeing me stand with Roman. I was his mate, and he was mine. Just because we hadn't made things official didn't mean we couldn't be together. I moved to his side as he answered Embry's question with full alpha confidence.

"We're going to use the portal spell right here in the office. Jack and Vaughn will be in charge of the pack while we're gone. This will be quick either way it goes—no more than a day. Our goal is to get Sam back the first time, but if we need a more thought-out plan, we will come back. Nobody needs to be a hero today." Roman's pointed gaze turned to Embry.

"I'd be more worried about your mate than myself, but don't worry, I'll keep an eye on her." Embry winked, but Roman didn't find it at all funny.

He turned toward me, and I held my hands in the air. "Hey, I have no plans of being a hero."

His stiff nod told me he didn't believe either of us, but unless he wanted to loop more people in on what was happening, Roman didn't really have a choice.

"Once we get through the portal, we'll arrive in Sydney, about half a mile from the stone holding Sam and other trapped souls that have been in there for who knows how long, powering the dark magic of the witches. We are not equipped to free the others, but it will be good to keep our eyes open and learn what we can. I'll pass on what we find to the local groups and let them handle it. First and foremost, though, we get Sam back."

Jack nodded. "Your plan is going to work, Son. You're a strong alpha, and the pull will be hard for Sam to resist as long as you're not interrupted."

Vaughn handed Embry a couple of small blades. "Try not to lose these ones this time, will you?"

She smirked. "At least when I lost the last set, it was because they were stuck in that vamp's junk."

"True. If you can do that again, I'll make you all the blades you need."

Vaughn threw two at me and miraculously, I caught them.

"What the fuck, Vaughn?" Roman snapped. "You could have stabbed her!"

The beta wasn't at all fazed. "Just making sure her reflexes are working before you go."

The four-inch daggers were sheathed with a thin black case, so I tucked each one into my back pockets. "The blades were covered, so I would have been fine either way," I said, hoping to calm Roman before we left.

He didn't seem to care. "Do something like that

again and we're going to have a problem."

Vaughn straightened and nodded, smart enough to know when enough was enough.

"We're leaving before I change my mind," Roman announced and pulled a vial of murky blue liquid from his pocket. He grabbed my hand and walked toward the back wall of his office before releasing his hold on me.

"Step back a pace or two," he warned before uncorking the vial and smashing it against the ground.

Sparks flickered on the hardwood floor, then died out as the liquid pooled into a puddle, doing nothing more. Disappointment filled me as I leaned forward to get a closer look. "Was it supposed to do somethi—"

Before I could finish, the sparks reignited, and smoke started to fill the room. Roman grabbed on to me before I could back away any further, and Embry was at my side within seconds.

"On the count of three, we all step through together," Roman said, and Embry grabbed my other hand.

"One, two, three!"

Within the blink of an eye, comfortably warm sunshine was streaming over us, and I inhaled the fresh salty air. I might not have missed my job in Sydney or the time change that made us skip into the future by half a day, but I sure as hell missed the country itself.

"We need to move in case someone is around. If a witch is near, she'll have sensed the surge of power.

Cait, try not to let any of your energy out," Roman said as he pulled us toward a sidewalk.

We'd landed behind a store, and there was nothing more than a dumpster and empty pallets around us. When we stepped onto the sidewalk, I wondered why my wolf had been so quiet.

Hey, Wolfette. You doing okay? I asked.

First off, quit calling me that. Wolf spirits don't normally have names, but if your odd human mind needs one to feel better, you can call me Adira. And to answer your question, yes, I'm fine. I'll be there when you need me. The longer we're together, the less we will feel the need to talk. Our thoughts will become one, as will our actions.

Adira. I like the sound of that. Thank you for sharing it with me and thank you for telling me. I'll leave you alone.

She didn't reply, and I wasn't sure if I should be offended. Maybe when we weren't trying to free another shifter from a freaking rock, I could ask Embry about how she handled things with her wolf.

Roman kept a tight hold on my hand as we entered a well-populated area—one I was familiar with. It wasn't the same beach I'd met Roman at, but it was close to it. Embry moved ahead of us, keeping about a twenty-foot distance.

"Shouldn't we stay together?" I asked.

"She's scouting for us. Don't worry, I won't let her out of my sight," Roman answered.

He was in full alpha mode, and it was interesting to watch him as his eyes constantly moved and his muscles tightened with every step we took, but I didn't observe for long.

I followed my instincts as Adira had advised and tried to mimic Roman. Every person was suspicious, yet they all seemed very human to me. I cleared my mind, taking a deep breath, and stopped focusing on the individuals. Instead, I searched for what didn't belong.

Roman didn't want me to use my energy, but I wasn't sure how else I was supposed to help. I sure as hell didn't tag along so I could stand by and do nothing.

Adira's presence made itself known as she pushed forward. Not forceful enough that I thought she was trying to make us shift, but enough that my sense of smell and my eyesight were suddenly a hundred times better than they had ever been.

We won't draw unwanted attention using this minimal amount of energy, Adira said, easing my worries.

I took a deep inhale and immediately regretted it as the stench of garbage from a nearby business assaulted me, as well as the body odors of those who had been out under the sun for more than a little while already.

Ignoring that and the things that belonged, I tried to focus deeper. I found nothing out of the ordinary until I saw Embry turn around, eyes wide and spinning to lean against a railing.

Roman stopped, swinging me around until I collided with his chest. He smiled down at me, cupping both of my cheeks and leaning. "Embry spotted two witches headed our way. They're going to recognize us as wolves. Let's hope nothing more and that they move on," he whispered.

I stiffened in his hold, but like an experienced pro, he kept up the act, raising his voice. "How about we ditch the guard dog?"

"How do you suppose we get rid of her?" I asked, trying to keep the tremble out of my voice.

He leaned close, speaking so low I shouldn't have been able to hear him. "They've stopped about ten feet behind us. I'm going to kiss you, and then we're going to run, and I need you to giggle like you're having the time of your life."

Roman did exactly as he said. His lips moved from my ear, down my cheek, finding a home at my mouth. I wrapped my arms around his neck, pressing closer to him and kissing him back with all I had.

Several seconds later, he pulled away from me and whispered louder than before, "Now!"

We sprinted away from where we wanted to be, and I had no idea where we were going. I wanted badly to turn back and see where Embry was, but I didn't want to screw anything up. Roman nudged me, and I remembered I was supposed to be acting the part of a love-struck wolf.

I giggled as requested and squeezed his arm hard as we raced through the crowds. We ended up behind another building, hiding next to a stack of boxes that appeared to have just been delivered.

Roman held me tightly against him, his body tense as we waited to see if anyone followed us. My heart was pounding out of my chest, but my wolf's subtle presence was enough to keep me calm.

She'd come a long way throughout the day. There was still an arrogance about her that I secretly loved, but she was more supportive of my choices. Hopefully, things would continue to get easier from here on out.

"They didn't follow us, but they're keeping a close eye on Embry. We'll have to return tonight instead of trying to do this during the day," Roman said.

"Won't there be more of them at night?" I asked.

He nodded. "But there will be less people, making it easier to use our abilities without detection if needed."

Said the person who didn't have glowing purple magic.

Roman gripped my elbows, and I met his intensity with a wave of my own. We'd gotten lucky with the witches not following us. I didn't need to be a supernatural my whole life to understand that.

As emotions increased between us, there was no acting needed. I pushed up onto my tiptoes, and he met me halfway. Our tongues danced, and a calmness immediately settled over me.

Never again would I fight the feelings he managed to draw from me. I still wasn't a fan of having choices taken from me, but I was beginning to see what Roman and I shared as the gift it was intended to be.

13

CAIT

Embry had thrown a fit about our "disappearance" to keep up the show we'd started in front of the witches, and we headed to a hotel nearby. None of them followed us as we moved through the crowded city I'd only just been in the month before.

We were near the beach I'd first met Roman at, and I couldn't believe how much my life had changed since then. So many things I'd never expected, yet I was eager for more.

Gaining my wolf spirit had changed everything for me all over again, but this time it allowed me to see things from a different perspective and made accepting the unknown a hell of a lot easier.

Roman checked us in and got one room with two beds. Though, I hoped we weren't there long enough to use them.

My skin tightened and my wolf perked up. I glanced

around and then nudged Embry as Roman led the way to the room. "Does something feel off to you?"

She shook her head. "Like what?"

"I don't know. Maybe it's just being back in Australia," I said, then reached out to Adira. *What about you?*

This is the first time you've been around the public and had your full abilities. You're sensing the other supernaturals around, the wolf replied.

So, people like us just roam around everywhere and humans have no idea?

Not normally. Sydney is a hot spot for magic users, as are New Orleans, Paris, and a few other major cities.

That was information I needed to tuck away for future use. I wanted to know more, but it wasn't time to be distracted.

We got on the elevator and I still felt off-kilter, so I stared out the doors while Roman and Embry talked about what we needed to do while we waited.

A woman dressed in all black with bright blue-and-purple hair caught my attention. She glared at me until a blond man tugged on her arm. The elevator doors closed before I could see which way they went. I didn't like it.

"We'll go out for dinner and see how things are then. We can also gauge how busy the nightlife is going to be," Embry said.

"My favorite Vietnamese restaurant is near the area we were before. More of a hole-in-the-wall type place. We can get a good look at things from there," I offered as we exited the elevator and headed down the hallway.

Embry rubbed a hand over her stomach. "Oh, I remember pictures of food from there. We're definitely doing that."

"We're not here to sightsee, Embry," Roman grumbled as he opened the door to our room.

The room was nothing fancy. Two queen beds, a mini fridge, bathroom, and basically, all of the things I'd expect, but something still felt off.

My hands rubbed over my arms as I looked around. Maybe it was too soon for me to be venturing into the world with my abilities. My wolf seemed confident we'd be able to handle our own and I'd just blindly trusted her. Now, I was beginning to second-guess things.

There was a soft tap on the door, and my stomach twisted. Adira surged to the surface, her awareness on high alert as well. *We weren't expecting guests,* she said.

Embry strode to the door and peeked through the hole. "It's a guy in a white polo and khaki shorts. Maybe he works here?"

Roman glanced at me and then went to the door himself. There was another knock. "Sir, you forgot your, um, breakfast vouchers," the man said from the other side.

"We don't need them," Roman replied back without opening the door.

"Can you just take them? It would make my life a whole lot easier," he said.

Embry shrugged, but I didn't like it.

"Don't answer the door," I said right as Embry did so.

The man was shoved aside, and the woman I'd seen from the elevator stormed through, magic swirling around her. She pointed at me. "What are you?"

Roman stepped between us. "That's none of your damn business, Lucinda."

She stepped closer to Roman as the guy with her closed our door. "I know you. You were on the islands recently."

"I was, and I left because your business is not mine, just as mine isn't yours. Now, leave," Roman demanded.

Lucinda, as he'd called her, peeked around at me with a raised brow. "Do you always let him speak for you?"

"Come on, Lucy. These people aren't our problem. We're only here for the day, and it's the first time we've left Fae Islands together like this. I thought you were going to show me all there was to love about this world," the man said, still staying near the door.

"Shush, Finnigan. There's something about this one. After what we went through, you can't blame me for being curious."

The man stepped forward, holding his hand out to Roman. "I'm Finn, not Finnigan. Lucinda is still on high alert after the issues we had on the islands. We've only just gotten away, and it seems a bit odd to run into someone we can't identify within the first hour of our arrival."

Embry moved near me as Roman took Finn's offered hand. I wasn't nervous anymore, but I didn't think these people were here to help us, either.

"I'm a wolf shifter," I finally said, staring at Lucinda.

"Is that so? Show me your claws, then," she replied.

I laughed. "I don't think so. I know nothing about you."

"Maybe I'll just hunt down Beatrix and get the answers I want. She's on my shitlist anyway," Lucinda said, and my jaw dropped a little that the newcomer somehow knew we were working with the witch.

"We're all here for our own reasons. None that have anything to do with each other, so why don't we just part ways and call it good?" Embry said.

"I agree with the female wolf," Finn added.

"No offense, dear, but nobody asked either of you." Lucinda turned toward Roman. "I don't want problems with you, Alpha. You caused none on my lands and I'm not trying to cause them here, but I sensed things are off balance in these parts as soon as we arrived, and I'm wondering if I've just stumbled upon the reason for the chaos."

Roman stepped into her personal space, looking down on the woman. "You're fae. Stick to your own world's problems."

She grinned. "I happen to like Earth better, so I don't think I will."

I moved in closer, annoyed with this whole situation

and ready to move past it. If Lucinda and Finn meant us harm, they'd have done something already.

"I am a wolf shifter, but no, I won't shift for you. I wasn't born a wolf and my magic isn't the same as the others. Happy now?" I crossed my arms, holding my head high even though the woman was several inches taller than me and probably a whole lot more powerful.

We could take her, Adira chimed in, making me smirk.

"Something funny, wolf?" Lucinda asked.

"Just me. So, are you going to leave us alone now?"

She glanced back at Finn, who seemed bored out of his mind, then at Roman and me. "Why are you here?"

"To find a friend," I said, not lying but also not giving all of the information.

Lucinda glared at me, her iridescent hair moving with the power I could feel flowing from her. "Very well. Try not to cause too much trouble. I'd prefer to enjoy my first proper visit back to Earth without work. Though, there is something cathartic about removing annoyances from this world. Don't tempt me to mix business with pleasure."

Finn pulled on her arm with a heavy sigh. Something told me he was constantly having to get her out of precarious situations and equal parts loved and hated his role.

Embry moved to open the door and helped push them along. Roman was tense at my side and vibrating with anger.

Once the door was closed, he inhaled deeply before

turning to me. "You can't tell people what you are. It's not safe."

I patted his chest. "Clearly, they can tell I'm not normal all on their own. It's better to give a version of the truth than draw more attention. I didn't get good vibes from her, but they weren't malicious either. It was better to get her gone as quickly as possible."

"I agree with Cait. Lucinda is known for being an uncaring hard-ass. That's the first time I've ever met her, but I've certainly heard plenty about the fae from her stay in LA," Embry said.

Roman gathered me into his arms. "How the hell am I supposed to keep you safe?" His words were murmured into my ear and mixed with so many emotions. I hated that he felt so out of sorts and that there was nothing I could do about it except stay hidden, which wasn't an option I was willing to consider.

"You just have to trust that my wolf is more capable than we know yet. I'm trying this new thing where I don't overthink every aspect of what's being thrown at me. You should do the same."

His body shook with forced laughter. "While I appreciate how open you've been since coming back, I'm not sure that's the best philosophy to have in our world."

I shrugged, pushing back to stare up at him. "As far as I can tell, it hasn't led me astray yet. I promise to listen to you and Embry, but I'm also my own person. I might not always do as suggested."

"Ha! That's an understatement," Embry said, but I ignored her, wanting to know how Roman felt about my words.

I wasn't going to be controlled. Just because he'd grown up in the supernatural world, didn't mean he'd always know better. I might be willing to give the bond a chance, but I wouldn't do it at the expense of losing who I was as a person.

"You're going to be the best and worst parts of my life," he groaned, and I smiled triumphantly.

"That's the way to see things," I said before pulling away completely. I didn't want Embry to constantly feel like a third wheel by being attached to Roman the entire time we were together.

Embry let out a heavy sigh. "It's going to be a long day cooped up in here."

"And why can't we venture out?" I asked.

"Like you so politely pointed out, other supernaturals are going to know you're different, and we don't need the witches getting too curious. Honestly, we're lucky they didn't follow us the first time," Roman answered.

"Don't they make a cloaking spell or something I could use?" I asked, trying to remember things from books I'd read that I hoped like hell were true.

"They do and you could if we had thought of that before Beatrix left. I doubt we'll be seeing much of her after this. She has never interfered in wolf business this much before. Most of the supernaturals keep to their own kind to avoid crossing any lines," Roman said.

"What kind of lines? Are there rules I should know about?" I probably needed a Supernatural 101 class, but as far as I knew, that didn't exist, so asking questions now was better than finding out answers after it was too late.

Embry plopped onto the small couch and kicked her feet up on the coffee table as I took a seat on one of the beds. Roman still stood, his big frame taking up too much of the room as Embry answered my question.

"The biggest thing is to try to avoid other supernaturals. It draws a lot of attention to see a shifter with a vampire or fae. Witches live by their own rules most of the time and get away with it, so it's not unusual to see one where they don't belong, but never on a long-term basis."

"Why do the witches have so much more power?" I asked.

"Because they're like ants, and they're everywhere. If they wanted to take charge of the council, they could. Thankfully, rules aren't really their thing, and as long as they're left alone, they don't make trouble for the rest of us," Roman answered this time as he poured himself a drink from the mini-bar.

It was the first time I'd seen him so out of sorts, and I felt bad that I was likely the cause of his disarray.

"Are there more than vampires, shifters, witches, and fae?" I asked next.

Embry nodded. "There are elves, but their population is dying out. Along with pixies, dwarfs, and a handful of others. If you ever see any of those, you know shit is about to hit the fan."

I spent another hour asking questions I thought might be helpful, and Embry tossed out information I wouldn't have thought to ask about, like how the council has to approve of interspecies relationships.

Apparently, they weren't forbidden, but the council controlled how many hybrids were out in the world since it was never guaranteed what kind of magic the offspring might be born with. In a way, it made sense to me, but it also sounded like an abuse of power.

I ended up having more questions than answers by the time we were done, but I also felt better about what to expect going against the witches to get Sam back.

She was Roman's best friend and his family. We'd do whatever it took to get her home safe. I just hoped I was as ready as my wolf had made me feel for what came next.

14

ROMAN

I was an alpha, for fuck's sake. I shouldn't have been this shaken, but between having Cait out in the open, Lucinda showing up, and knowing Sam was stuck in the damned witch boulder, I was losing it.

While Embry and Cait chatted about things I was already fully aware of, I took time to calm myself and focus on what I could control, like when we left, where we went, and how I planned to keep Cait safe.

We might not be bonded yet, but her wolf doesn't seem like the type who wants to be protected, my wolf said.

Yeah, well, she doesn't have a choice.

I'm not sure it's going to work that way, and it's better you understand that now.

My hands ran through my hair for the hundredth time as I thought about his words. Cait had never wanted to be controlled. Her wolf seemed to be full of confidence and, according to Embry, for good reason.

Every part of me wished I'd gone to train with Cait,

even though she'd asked for time alone. Seeing what she could do might have made me feel better.

That's a lie, my wolf deadpanned.

He was probably right, but we couldn't change things now. All we could do was prepare for what was coming next.

And what's that? he asked.

We get to the stone and pull Sam out with an alpha command.

If that doesn't work and things get out of hand, what's the backup plan, besides trying to get the hell out of Sydney?

I didn't have any plans beyond getting in and out as quickly as possible and he knew it. My frustration level was climbing, and I needed more action instead of sitting here doing nothing.

"Enough," I snapped at Cait and Embry.

Two sets of heated eyes turned my way.

"Having a Q&A session right now isn't going to help Sam," I added.

"It will if Cait is as informed as she can be," Embry replied.

She had a point, but it wasn't good enough.

"No. I've been thinking, and we need more options. Ones the two of you can assure me that you'll be on board with." Using my alpha role against my wolves wasn't something I liked to do, but if it meant keeping the two of them safe—even if they weren't happy about it—I would do whatever it took.

I stood between them, looking down and settling into the role of the man I needed to be then. Not someone's mate, not a friend, not anything other than an alpha.

"This is how things are going to work. We will leave here and get dinner. We will not sightsee on the way, and you will eat quickly. Once the sun is set, we will head to the beach where the boulder is. We will spend some time getting a feel for the scene. When all seems clear, I will go to the rock while the two of you keep watch. From a distance."

I could see the ire rising in both of them. Embry had always been a good wolf, but there was a reason she was part of our ranking pack members, and that reason wasn't helpful when I needed to be in control.

Cait didn't move or say a word, but her eyes spoke volumes as her wolf rose to the surface, prepared to challenge me, but also respecting my role as her mate and an alpha.

"Once there, I will draw Sam's body out with the alpha command. Like Beatrix said before, it's our best chance to get her back without drawing much attention. We should be shielded in that area from humans, and given Sam hasn't been there too long, my hope is that she's still coherent enough to be eager about getting free."

"And if that doesn't work?" Cait asked with a raised brow.

"Then, we will leave, and I will put a call in for back-up." I had other supernaturals I could call on. Beatrix wasn't the only witch I knew, and there was an alpha in Australia who I could call in a favor to. He had to have resources that would allow us to get Sam. For now, I was trying to involve the fewest amount of people until we had an idea of what we were dealing with.

I didn't need people poking their nose around in my business when it came to Cait, and Sam didn't like others involved in her missions. We'd try things the easiest way first and hope it didn't all go to shit in my face.

"You'd call Sal?" Embry asked about the Australia alpha with a bit of shock.

"He's not that bad," I answered.

She nearly choked. "Right. I've only met him once, but that was enough for me after seeing him wrestle with an alligator just for fun."

"What if one of us gets hurt?" Cait pressed.

"Then, we use the portal spell from Beatrix and get the hell out of here." I pulled the potion from my pocket and handed it to Cait. "I want you to keep it, and if things get too bad, then you need to leave us and get Vaughn. He'll know what to do."

Cait's eyes darkened, and her lip curled as she tilted her head up, meeting my eyes. Never once had she shied away from matching my stare, and that worried me. She was stronger than she knew.

"The chances of that being necessary aren't high, but I want the option there if needed. As soon as we have an opening, we will take it and be out of here before anyone knows what we've done," I said, hoping to appease the wolf rising to the surface.

Cait's hands shook as she fought for control. She wasn't ready for this, no matter how powerful she was. The kind of pure magic she held inside needed to be harnessed and well-used before going into battle. I'd made a mistake by letting Cait come with us. Embry and I could have handled it, but I'd let my heart make the decision. Not the smartest thing I'd done lately.

Regardless, we were here, and Sam needed us. Cait's wolf was experienced enough for now, and I'd make sure the next time we left on a mission, there was nothing to worry about.

///

I'd come to the conclusion that spending an extended amount of time alone with Cait and Embry was not the wisest thing I'd ever done. They went on and on about the supernatural world, shopping, vacations, and everything that had nothing to do with the mission.

It was non-stop talking, even after I'd snapped at them about it not being helpful. I'd hardly had a moment to think clearly, but night was near, and it was time to head for the restaurant. Both Cait and Embry were starving, and the hotel didn't have room service. So, when the topics changed to food, I'd had enough.

"Let's go," I said and grabbed onto Cait's hand on my way toward the door. Heat traveled up my arm and straight to my heart. I sighed, realizing the problem hadn't been the stress of what we needed or the unknown of what could happen. It had been not being physically with my mate.

Cait was my balance in this world. Holding her and keeping her close only made me stronger, and I'd let the intensity of my fears make me forget that.

As long as I had Cait, my mate, my other half, everything would be fine. We'd get Sam, and we'd all make it home. Everything was going to be fine.

Famous last words, my wolf muttered, but I ignored him. I didn't need doubts. I needed to see the outcome I wanted and make it happen.

We headed out of the hotel, and I kept an eye out for Lucinda. I didn't need her kind of trouble, and I had been surprised to see her so soon. I hadn't heard their battles ended, but then again, the fae didn't often share their business and I didn't make a point to ask about it.

Either way, I was glad when she'd left with Finn. He seemed capable enough, but still.

Outside, the air was cooling down and I took a deep breath. Everything here was clearer than the big cities in the states. I'd always enjoyed visiting the massive island, but only for short times. Being away from my pack for too long made my chest tighten.

It was a Wednesday night, and the streets of Sydney were quieter than I expected—something I wouldn't complain about. If things got out of hand, the less people around, the better.

Cait's hand stayed tucked into mine, and I wondered if she felt the draw to me like I did to her. Did my touch give her the same boost hers did to me? I wanted to press her with so many questions, but I was still treading carefully.

I'd only just gotten her back, and even if she seemed more open to the ideals of my world, a part of me didn't want to push her with too much too fast.

Until she wore my scent and we were officially mated, I'd act with caution. There wasn't a future I was willing to accept any longer without Cait by my side. At one point, I'd been stupid enough to believe I could survive by merely keeping an eye on her from a distance, but after losing Cait... I knew that would never be an option.

"It's up here on the right. We can get a seat on the back patio and see the beach," Cait said as we walked swiftly down the sidewalk.

We entered the small Vietnamese restaurant and followed an older woman down a narrow dingy hallway that led to a door about ready to fall off its hinges. This place was the poster child for "hole-in-the-wall" diners.

She pointed to one of three metal tables on the patio and tossed some menus down before disappearing back inside.

I chose the seat with the best view of the beach, and Cait had been right. I could see the curve before the boulder we needed to get to, and this would be a decent spot to search for people we wanted to avoid.

I wasn't all that hungry, so I let Cait and Embry order for all of us as I kept watch. Waters were brought out first, followed by a thick, clear soup I wanted nothing to do with. Trays of food kept appearing after that until there was no room left on the table.

The only thing that looked appetizing to me were strips of steak. There were a lot of soups, noodles, and vegetables that I would be avoiding.

Cait and Embry dug in, but I noticed frown lines on Cait's face as she looked around the table. "What's wrong?" I asked.

"This is horrible. Why is it horrible?" she asked, voice tinged with sadness.

"Your body went through..." I had a hard time letting myself remember that Cait had died not too long ago, "a lot of changes. You might not have the same tastes anymore."

"Well, that's disappointing," she said, staring longingly at the food that likely wouldn't be eaten.

Embry reached for more. "I don't know what's wrong with your wolf, but mine loves this stuff."

Or maybe it would all get devoured.

I reached for Cait's leg under the table. "Stick to the meats. It might help."

She nodded and did just that while I glanced over the beach again. "I've never seen Sydney so quiet," I said.

Cait turned and looked around. "Might have been too hot today? It's also a weeknight."

She made good points, but I could see by the way her eyes kept moving over the beach, she didn't like the emptiness, either.

I gave Embry a five-minute warning to finish

shoveling food down her throat, then paid the bill. We left down the back stairs and headed toward the beach. Cait stayed next to me and made the first move to grab my hand once we hit the sand. My wolf rumbled in contentment.

I squeezed her hand, pulling her closer to my side, and soaked up the electrical current of magic that flowed between us. A dark chill ran down my spine at the thought of anything ever happening to Cait again. The thoughts put my mind back on focus.

It was time to get Sam and head back home.

15

CAIT

There was something eerie about the beach we were walking on. I'd felt it the moment we left the hotel, and I tried to push the negative thoughts aside, but they persisted. Something wasn't right, but I didn't know enough to find the words to explain how I felt.

"Are you okay?" Roman asked as the sky darkened around us.

"I think so. My wolf seems fine," I said. Adira had been quiet, but her presence was alert and ready. She was letting me lead while offering her strength, something I hadn't expected so soon from her, considering how much attitude she'd thrown my way at first.

Apparently, I just needed to show Roman a little love and it was smooth sailing with her. I didn't let myself think too long on how asinine that thought was. My wolf was powerful in her own right. From the sounds of it, she didn't need a mate, but her choices seemed directly tied to Roman.

You'll understand one day. I shouldn't have been so hard on you. I can see you're trying now, Adira said with only the slightest amount of spite in her tone.

Now wasn't the time for a heart-to-heart, so I let her comment go and refocused on our surroundings. Roman's paces slowed and I tensed.

"Why are we stopping?" I asked.

"The boulder is just around the corner. We don't know what we're going to find there. I need you both to listen to me every step of the way. Until I give the all-clear, the two of you will wait at this point." Roman pointed to the edge of the cliff we were walking again.

I didn't like the thought of him going ahead without us, but I kept my comments to myself. For the time being, at least.

"What happens if there is a coven of witches around that corner?" Embry asked.

"If there was, we would have sensed them by now," Roman replied confidently.

I gave him a gentle shove forward. "Let's get this over with then, before that changes."

He nodded but moved back in to wrap his hand around my neck, garnering my full attention. "Listen to your wolf, and don't be too prideful to leave if things get to be too much. Embry and I will be just fine as long as you're safe."

Roman's lips pressed against my forehead, and he was walking away before I could respond. I didn't want to consider the possibility of leaving the two of them behind. I was positive I wasn't capable of such a thing, but I didn't say as much. Roman didn't need the added stress of my stubbornness right then.

We followed him to the peak and stood just far enough away that we could see his path. There, in the middle of the sandy beach, was a thirty-foot-tall boulder that stretched about ten feet wide. The hairs on my arms stood, and I shivered.

"It's the magic from the witches. Normally, they draw from their ancestors, but this rock is powered by the dead, making it even more potent," Embry whispered.

"Why hasn't anyone destroyed it?" I asked.

"Because to destroy something that contains that much power would have devastating results. The magic has to go somewhere when it's broken. Whoever dared to demolish the boulder would likely die from being bombarded with the power."

I nodded, glancing around. The ocean's waves were crashing onto the shore just five-or-so yards away. The night sky was clear, and the air still held warmth in it from the day. Everything seemed calm, but still, I thought it was too quiet.

My eyes watched Roman as he moved confidently along the beach and held a dagger tucked at his side. If he was worried still, he hid the feelings well.

I called back to Embry to comment about the eerie silence, but the words never left my mouth as I watched Roman disappear from thin air, leaving behind his weapon that dropped to the sand with an inaudible thud. "Where the hell did he go?" My voice was rough as rage consumed me.

I was already fully aware of the strong feelings I held for Roman, but the moment he vanished, every ounce of them hit me square in the chest with an intensity I hadn't expected. My mate couldn't be seen, which didn't work well for me.

"I don't know. Just give him a minute," Embry replied, staring hard at the empty beach, as if that would make Roman reappear.

That didn't work for me. Fury rose inside me faster than I could control it. I knew I was supposed to be careful with my power, but something was wrong, and we needed to help Roman.

"Cait," Embry warned. "You need to calm down."

"That's the exact opposite of what I need right now." I took a step forward, and Embry hissed from connecting with my energy when she tried to jerk me back.

"Well, that was rude," she said as her steps matched my stride. "What's your plan?"

"Find Roman."

"And then?"

"Make sure he's okay," I said.

"And then?"

I glared at her, annoyed. "See how we can help, and if you say 'and then' one more time, I'm going to kick you."

She smirked. "Just trying to make you see reason.

We had a plan. One that Roman made. We should stick to it."

I waved my hand flippantly. "Well, Roman's not here, is he? Plan went to shit, and we're making a new one unless you think your alpha is fine on his own contending with whatever made him disappear."

My words finally struck home. People, even the supernatural kind, didn't just *poof* out of existence. Someone was messing with us, and I couldn't leave Roman alone to deal with it himself—no matter what he'd said before about me leaving them behind.

"Fine, but I'm going to say you forced me when he's angry," Embry replied as we continued forward.

I didn't care what she said once we got Roman back. All I knew was that the closer we got to the spot he disappeared at, the worse my gut twisted. My steps slowed as I tried to see what wasn't there. I was new to this whole magic thing, but I knew we were surrounded by something sinister and powerful.

"Is the pulse I feel coming from the rock?" I asked.

"I don't know. Most likely. It's darker than anything I've ever experienced," Embry answered.

We proceeded with caution, but no amount of carefulness prepared us for what came next.

After three more steps, I tried to suck in a deep breath as the air pulled from my lungs and we were thrown into a completely different scene.

"The witches must have an illusion around the boulder. What we were seeing before wasn't reality. This is," Embry hissed, anger filling her words.

"It was a set-up," I said, trying to find Roman among the dark faces before us.

"Most likely," Embry muttered.

As I took in the scene before me, I reached out to my wolf, *We're in over our heads.*

No, this is called hands-on training.

You knew what we were getting into, didn't you? I asked

I had an idea. Now, focus.

That sneaky little wench. So much for thinking we were turning a new leaf and going to be getting along well. The witches hadn't been the only ones preparing for a set-up.

The sky was even darker above us, and the air held a chill I'd never felt in Australia before. There were a dozen-or-so people spread out in front of the rock that was just the size I'd seen before, but it was making a horrendous groaning sound, and thin plumes of smoke rose from it, along with the etched in screaming faces I recognized from Beatrix's magical image of the stone.

I couldn't see a single face beneath the hooded robes the witches wore, but I could see the glow of a silver ring around what I assumed to be their eyes. Slowly, each of their hands raised at the same time and they took a synchronized step forward.

Roman was nowhere to be seen, and I began to panic.

"What are we supposed to do?" I asked Embry with a hushed voice. The witches were a decent distance away from us, but I didn't assume that would last long.

"We can't go back. The forcefield they have up only

lets people through as the witches please. We're stuck in here until we fight our way out or they release us."

My eyes scanned the coming horde, searching for any sight of Roman. On my third pass, I finally caught him stuck to the side of the boulder. His back was pressed against the rock, jaw tense, and arms sprawled back by a greater force.

Embry must have noticed him at the same time I did, because she let out a nasty snarl before narrowing her gaze at the advancing witches.

"Give us the girl and you can have your alpha. We have no desire for trouble with the wolves," all of the voices said at once.

From what I could tell, they were all female and synced together in a creep-tastic sort of way.

"Not a chance in hell," Embry replied.

"You can have the other wolf back, too. We have no need for her," they added.

"Be ready to shift. You won't stand a chance without the speed of your wolf," Embry murmured, her arms shaking and ready to act.

I nodded, fighting off my own vibrations. I might have been capable of some cool shit back at the pack, but facing down a dozen dark witches was nothing like playing around with my best friend in the safety of a wolf pack that didn't want to kill me.

We are more powerful than even the witches realize. Don't think. Just act, Adira said, and I took her words to heart, because she was my only hope of getting Roman back. He hadn't given up on me when I'd been taken, and I wasn't going to walk away from him now when he needed us.

"One more step and we will be forced to act," the witches echoed.

Fear slithered along my exposed skin, but I ignored it and focused on one thing: getting past the dozen witches that seemed to have an interest in me so I could free Roman from the damn rock.

"Shift," Embry said right before she transformed from woman to beast at my side.

I did the same, sighing as the euphoria of power washed over me. I'd still been worried shifting would hurt, but just like before, there was only a high that came over me. Once I was on four paws, I shook out my longer fur, letting my tail swish back and forth as I lowered my head, searching for the best way to get to our mate.

Adira was right. I couldn't think. Humans thought, and I wasn't human anymore. I needed to rely on my predator instincts and trust they would serve me well. Fighting who I'd become was only going to make my failure more of a possibility.

There was an even spacing of two feet between each witch. With my wolf eyes, we could see sparks of magic connecting them all. We'd either have to break their connection or attempt to leap over them.

If we don't break the connection, we'll never get past them, Adira said.

I had a feeling that was the case, I replied, giving another glance at Roman. His hands were submerged in the rock and his eyes locked on mine. They were bright with a wrath I recognized from when he'd first found me.

Roman didn't like losing control any more than I did.

Embry bounded forward, heading for the right side while I went for the left. Dark circles of magic were flung at us, but my wolf was fast—faster than their movements. I heard a yelp from Embry, but my wolf wouldn't turn her head.

The best way to help them both is to rip the witches apart, she said, and as much as I hated her reasoning, my gut said she was right.

One of the orbs nicked my tail, scorching the hairs at the end, and sent a current of torturous heat down my spine.

We ignored the pain and leaped between two of the witches. Their hands reached out, grabbing on to my fur. Two sets of nails dug into my skin. Shit, that had hurt more than I'd expected.

My wolf bit at the one closest, teeth sinking into their forearm and blood filling our mouth. I wanted to be disgusted, but there was no time. The more we fought against the first one, the more of an upper hand the other witch got.

Beads of magic traveled over my wolf form, and our movements slowed. Adira released the first witch and launched herself at the second. With one bite and a relentless head shake, blood that wasn't ours sprayed in the face of our opponent, but I still couldn't make out any identifying features besides the silver ring in their eyes.

Sharp nails raked across my wolf's face, one of them dangerously close to her eye. *It's time to show them the power they'll never have,* Adira said.

Energy flowed through us with speed and purpose. The trail of heat began in our chest, growing in strength before expanding through all my extremities, healing my wolf as it went. The purple hue around us grew brighter and stronger until it began to brighten the faces surrounding us.

There were now four witches hovered around my wolf, each of them with a shaved head and that silver ring around their black eyes. Skin tones ranged from fair to dark telling me they weren't blood-related, but most importantly, I was thankful they still had human faces. A part of me was picturing a nose-less psychopath.

Either way, they were still trying to kill us, and we had to get to Roman.

Embry's wolf howled, but it didn't sound like she was in pain, which caused a wave of relief to flow through me as my wolf created a barrier around us. She kept gathering power into our core, and our body was heating up.

I had no idea what she was doing, but I was paying attention to every move she made so I could assist in whatever way I was capable of. We were supposed to be one, yet I didn't feel that way. Maybe one day. For now, I was happy to let her take the lead and trust she would get us past these witches.

Dark magic, or what I assumed it to be, pressed down on us, and it took every effort to keep standing beneath the barrier we'd created. Even though we weren't physically being struck by the witches, their energy was still taking a toll on ours.

Push when I do, Adira said.

Instead of replying, I acted, and we shoved the power inside us out, directing it at the sparks of magic we could see connecting the witches. They screamed but didn't relent. If anything, our move seemed to empower them, which wasn't good.

Our barrier broke when we let out the burst of magic, and the witches piled down on us. My wolf's head twisted until her teeth latched on to anything deemed bite-worthy, then she jerked her head around several times before releasing and finding the next arm or torso or neck to attack.

Claws and teeth were our best defense in the moment as our pool of energy filled back up. The push of magic hadn't tired us out, but it wasn't never-ending, and we needed a moment.

Embry's howl cut through the screeching of the witches, a sound that seemed full of hope, but given my current predicament, I wasn't sure where her positivity was coming from.

The witches moved faster, their magic circling my wolf and pressing down on us. Breathing became harder, but we weren't giving up. We couldn't. There was too much at stake.

My wolf began to vibrate, and waves of heat rolled off of us, reminding me of the high friction energy I'd first used when I'd began training with Embry. Adira didn't seem familiar with this power, so I helped as much as I could by clearing my mind and focusing only on what we wanted most—to break the witches' connection.

Their hits kept coming, and while I could feel our energy draining, we weren't even close to done. Pain seared into our rear flank and another spot on our back, but I ignored the hurt and thought of nothing other than the heat I knew I could produce.

The witches' screeches got louder as they fought harder. I had no idea how many of them were on top of us now or where Embry was. As the heat around us burned hotter, the agony from our wounds rose tenfold.

We weren't going to be able to keep up with the output if the witches didn't yield. We had to find a way to be stronger than them.

A painful roar reached my ears and my heart stuttered.

It was Roman.

I knew without a doubt that my mate was hurting. That thought was all I needed to give more of myself than I thought I had left to offer.

16

CAIT

Purple heat moved in waves around my wolf as a deep howl ripped from our chest. We had to get to Roman. There was no more time to waste. If we lost him to the rock, I had no idea how we'd get him back, and that wasn't a scenario I wanted to find ourselves in.

"No!" the witches screamed around us as energy flowed freely. At first, I thought they'd attempt to take the power I was letting loose, but whatever had changed, turned on them in a good way for us.

The connection had visible fissures between the witches still attacking us. A couple of them stood back, trying to repair the damage I'd caused.

Good luck, bitches, I thought.

My wolf clawed her way through the three nearest to us, cutting deep where we could and ripping skin off as the opportunity arose.

One of the witches latched onto our front leg and hit us with something cold and empty. Energy immediately began to seep from us, and we tried to back away, but their hold was tight. Adira whipped her head back and snarled before lunging at the one holding us.

The move gave the other two an opportunity to attack our back, but there wasn't much we could do to avoid it without losing the fight completely.

Adira jumped as high as we could leap while being surrounded and found her mark on the witch's neck, tearing our teeth into the fragile skin and biting down with every bit of energy we had left.

Our claws dug into the magic user's chest while hands pulled at our long fur, trying to yank us back. We didn't relent, but neither did the witch. At least, not until our jaw clamped down tight and I heard the cracking of bone.

The magic surrounding us weakened instantly, and the ability to breathe became easier, but we weren't in the clear yet.

Adira spit the witch out and backed up as everyone else did, too. Embry's wolf joined us, covered in blood I hoped wasn't all hers. She nodded, and I searched for Roman. He was barely visible in the rock. We were running out of time to find a way to save him.

"Yield, or you will all die," a woman's voice sounded from one of the eight witches still standing.

Neither Embry nor I moved. We weren't leaving without Roman.

A form flew over us, and I assumed it was the witches striking once again, except a few of them tensed and began sending strings of magic into the night sky. Whatever was up there was too fast to hit, though.

I glanced at Embry. She was snarling and prepared to fight once more.

What is that? I asked Adira.

Either an enemy we're not prepared to fight or an ally. Let's hope for the latter.

Two of the witches disappeared, and I heard a dark chuckle echo around us. "Oh, come on. The party's just getting started," a man's voice added.

While the witches were distracted with the newcomer, I wanted to get Roman, and Adira didn't oppose. We darted around them and headed for the rock. Heavy magic pressed down on us, but instead of feeling suffocated by it, my energy began to increase.

Don't take the power in. It's not the kind we want, Adira said as we stood in front of Roman. *I can't help him in this form. You need to shift back.*

Without hesitation, I did as she suggested and was back on two feet within the blink of an eye. My hands reached out to Roman's chest that was still visible. "We're going to get you out."

His face was nearly embedded into the stone, so he couldn't talk, but the glare in his eyes spoke volumes.

Embry appeared at my side, a scratch on her cheek that was freshly bleeding. I had a quick thought to check myself for injuries but opted not to. Better not to concern myself with anything I couldn't fix at the moment.

"You need to call for him like he planned to do for Sam," Embry said.

"How the hell am I supposed to do that?"

"Use your bond. You might not be mated, but there is still a connection between the two of you. Find it and yank on that fucker before it's too late. No pressure, but you maybe have another minute before we're screwed."

We can do it. Just calm down and focus like you did when you created your own magic with the witches, Adira said.

Okay, I could do this. I had to do this. Roman and everyone else who cared about him were counting on me.

With a quick glance behind us, I saw a man dressed in all black with short brown hair, dark skin, and red eyes. "Is that…"

Embry forced me to face Roman again. "Don't think about that. I will worry about *him*."

Right. Don't stress about the vampire killing powerful witches just a few yards away. I could do that.

Closing my eyes, I pictured Roman and nothing else. I recalled the first time I saw him and the attraction I'd felt even then. I thought about our first kiss, the time at the river when he taught me how to skip a rock, and the fierceness of his touch when he'd finally found me.

Every thought and feeling warmed me from the inside out. On instinct, I reached my hand out without opening my eyes. My fingers mostly felt stone, but there was heat from Roman there underneath as well.

My focus remained on that, and the harder I thought about him, the more our connection strengthened. His heartbeat sounded in my ears and my own synced with him. My fingers dug into the rock, breaking pieces away as I grasped on to his shirt.

Minutes passed as I continued to pull on Roman, both literally and figuratively. Every time I felt the hold on him loosen, a burst of power filled me. The closer he got, the stronger I became.

"Almost free," Roman's voice murmured, but I didn't dare let that excite me.

I kept my eyes closed and my focus on nothing other than bringing Roman back to me.

My wolf cautioned me about something, but I wasn't listening to her any longer. I couldn't hear anything other than the heart that now owned mine. I needed it back at my side and safe.

Finally, warm arms encased me, and Roman's lips pressed against my ear. "Let go, Kitten. You did it. I'm okay. We're all okay."

I opened my eyes, blinded by my own magic. Heat circled around us, but both Roman and me were untouched.

Roman's hands cupped my cheeks. "You have to let go of the magic, Cait."

My brow pinched. I didn't know what he meant. It was mine, and I didn't want to give that power to the rock.

He shook me. Hard. "Now, Cait."

Adira was yelling at me, too, but I'd been blocking her out. Finally, I let her in. *You took on dark magic to free him. Give it back before it kills me, you idiot.*

Shit!

I had no idea how I was supposed to do that, but I shoved my hands out with palms facing up and shouted, "Out!", trying the most literal thing that came to mind.

Roman was at my side and guided me back toward the rock. "Place your hands on the boulder, and instead of soaking in the magic that is pulsing from it, shove your own toward it. The remaining dark magic in the stone will draw out the parts of it inside you."

Okay, that seemed easy enough. I pressed my palms to the hot surface—pretty convinced that when I pulled them away there would be burn marks—and drew on the new energy, willing it to follow the flow of my arms and enter the rock.

As soon as my power and the rock's collided, my muscles tightened and teeth clenched. This was painful as shit. My body grew tired quickly, and my shoulders started to sag.

"I can't hold you up without taking on the dark magic myself. You're almost done," Roman said, and I had no idea how he knew, but I was taking his word for it.

My forehead leaned against the boulder, and I focused on breathing while trying to distract myself. *How are you doing in there, Wolfie?*

I gave you a name to call me for a reason. I'm not fond of Wolfie. Or Wolfette.

She sounded just as tired as I felt. *Is this affecting you?*

Anything that negatively impacts you, does to me as well.

I'm sorry, I replied.

She grumbled. *Don't be. We got him back. That's most important. Now, we just need to find his cousin.*

Adira was right about that, which gave me an idea. I wasn't Sam's alpha, but I was tied to this rock and didn't appear to be going anywhere anytime soon.

Can we get her out? I asked.

No idea. You're welcome to try.

I heard shouts from behind me, but I ignored them as I did what felt natural. The power I'd been given was new to me, but at the same time, seemed more like a long-lost friend than a stranger. I wasn't afraid of it anymore. I wasn't concerned with what came next, only what was right in front of me.

The thought would have scared the hell out of the old me, but I didn't mind this new change. My hope was that it made whatever came next easier to handle with less freak-outs.

Hands latched on to my arms and waist, jerking me back and forth. Agony rocketed through me as the connection I'd formed to the boulder was disrupted. The magic source didn't want to let go of me. That wasn't something I'd expected.

I finally got free and ended up on top of Embry about ten feet from the rock. "What happened?" I asked as I rolled off of her.

"The boulder was absorbing you. Once the dark magic was gone from your body, you began to move closer and closer. What were you doing?"

"I was trying to get to Sam. I thought since I was connected to the power of the stone, it might be our best shot." Before I finished my sentence, Roman yanked me up from the sand, and his arms wrapped around me until I could barely breathe.

"You are going to be the death of me." His words were filled with an ache that cut right through my chest.

"I'm sorry."

Roman pulled back just far enough so that he could see my face. "You don't need to be sorry. You didn't know, and it was a good idea. Unfortunately, it didn't work."

"I told you there is no way to get her out of there. I've tried everything," a man from behind Embry said.

I'd forgotten about the newcomer toward the end of the fight. He'd handled the remaining witches and now had droplets of blood splattered on his chin. I shuddered, hoping he didn't find anything tasty about the three of us.

"Cait, this is Zeke. He's a vampire and has supposedly been working with Sam for a while now," Roman said with disdain.

Zeke bowed at me. "Lovely to meet you, Ms. Cait. I'm sorry it's under such circumstances."

"Uh, nice to meet you, too," I replied, taken aback by his politeness.

"He's over a century old and acts like it, too," Embry said, moving closer to me now that Zeke was facing the three of us.

His red-mahogany eyes brightened. "You're just

jealous of what I can do with all of the knowledge I've acquired in that time."

Embry gagged. "There will never be a day in my life when I am jealous of a bloodsucker."

Zeke nodded and kept the smirk on his face that drew out his strong cheekbones. "Whatever you say, Embry." He glanced at Roman. "How are we going to get Sam back?"

"*We*," Roman pointed between the three of us, "are going to figure it out ourselves. Sam has never mentioned you, so I don't trust you. I won't force you to go, considering I don't have time for that, but make a move toward us and you'll find out how hungry my wolf is."

The deep rumble of Roman's voice told me how serious he was. I had no desire to see the two of them fight, so I spoke before Zeke could say anything further. "How about you call for Sam like you planned to before everything went to hell? Can you sense her?" I asked.

Roman's jaw tightened, and I had my answer. Shit, maybe Zeke was right.

"I'll figure something out," Roman said, reaching for his phone.

"No, you won't, but luckily for you, I'm a curious bitch," a voice sounded just before Lucinda and Finn popped into existence.

Embry laughed. "It must be our lucky day. We've had the pleasure of hanging out with fae, witches, *and* a vampire." Sarcasm dripped from her every word as she glared at the newcomers.

"Easy, dog. I mean no harm. Sure, you ruined my very short break from Fae Islands, but there's something about that one I like." Lucinda pointed at me. "I'm willing to help you."

"Okay. Our friend is stuck in there. Can you get her out?" I asked without hesitation, because I had no idea how everyone else would receive her offer.

The vampire had already backed up several paces, and Roman's grip on me was nearly painful. She really must have some reputation.

"Normally, there is nothing I can do about witch spells, but this isn't ordinary magic I'm sensing. Whoever created this combined their powers with things that shouldn't be mixed. If I had more time, I'd call on someone to destroy it, but we don't."

"So, what do you have time for?" Embry asked.

Finn whispered something in the fae's ear that had her grinning. If a woman like her was happy about something, the rest of us probably didn't want to know why.

"Lucinda is a unique fae. She can tolerate the dark and light magic that is present here," Finn said as she spread her wings.

Holy mother-freaking wings.

There was no hiding my shock. When I'd heard fae were real, I'd pictured thin gossamer wings, but these were nothing of the sort. No, they were obsidian at the top, fading to charcoal color at the tips and made of feathers, but not the soft kind I'd want to pet. These ones would likely take my head off with no effort on her part.

The tips of them glinted in the moonlight as Lucinda shoved her colorful hair back. "How long has she been in there?"

"Four days," Zeke answered from behind us.

"Not an ideal situation, but it's workable," Lucinda murmured as she stepped closer to the rock. Before she did anything else, she glanced back at Roman. "Your friend might not be the same person when she comes out. Are you prepared to deal with that if so?"

"She is my wolf. I'm more than capable of doing what needs to be done, should the need arise."

Lucinda nodded, trusting Roman at his word—a courtesy he wouldn't have given her. Hell, I was even surprised he was letting the outspoken woman help at all, but just as she'd said about me, there was something about her I liked. I had a feeling there was a lot more to her than the clear joy she got from being a bitch.

Her wings spread out, extending a good six feet on both sides. They pulled forward as if cocooning her in, but instead pressed against the boulder. Her wings hardened, and it appeared as if the fae had anchored herself to the stone. Thick bands of teal magic swirled around the rock as Lucinda slowly entered the boulder. Somehow, her wings remained on the outside, and I held my breath as they began to shake.

Finn stepped closer, pressing his hand on the space between each wing extending from her back—the only part of Lucinda still showing. "Come on, Lucy. Grab the wolf and get out of there. This isn't the time to be curious."

His words were low, but my wolf hearing picked them up without effort. We all waited for what felt like eternity until a fissure in the stone opened up above where I assumed Lucinda's head would be.

Snarling and yelling could be heard as the opening got bigger. Then, finally, a very pissed-off Sam was tossed onto the sand.

Her previously platinum-blonde hair was covered in dirt and blood. Her clothes were ripped to the point that she might as well have not had any on, and her eyes were nearly black as she stared at all of us. There was a hesitation when her glare landed on Lucinda and Finn, then Zeke stepped forward and she lunged at him first.

I thought maybe they meant more to each other than anyone realized, but when I heard the snapping of teeth, I backed up several steps.

"Calm down, Samantha," Zeke demanded, which only infuriated her more.

I nudged Roman, who had followed me when I moved out of the way. "Aren't you going to do anything?"

He shrugged. "Clearly, he deserves it."

"Or she's not in her right mind and is going to regret hurting her friend, then be furious with you for not stopping her."

Roman considered my words and sighed. "I can't

believe there's a chance she's friends with a bloodsucker."

"And I wonder why she didn't tell you," I countered.

Embry joined us. "She's going to kill him."

"Who? Zeke or Roman?" I had a feeling it could be both if nobody did anything.

She grinned. "Good point."

Roman sighed and stepped forward. "Sam McIntyre, *stop*." The tone of his voice was so deep it echoed around us and caused bumps to rise on my arms. The words packed a punch, and I hoped he never tried to talk to me that way.

Sam paused in her attack on Zeke, who was cut deep in multiple places, but the wounds were healing quickly. She turned back toward us, eyes still black and a snout for a mouth, though the rest of her was still human. I wanted to turn away, but it was so creepy that I couldn't.

"Sam, let go of the vampire and submit." Roman's arms were crossed, and he moved another step forward.

Something told me that the words "Sam" and "Submit" never went together.

Lucinda sighed heavily. "You're either going to need to put her down or let me help again. You're lucky Finnigan thinks you all are good people."

I laughed. "I thought you were only here because you're a curious bitch?"

She winked at me. "I knew I liked you." Then, she lowered her voice. "It's a bit of both."

Lucinda moved toward Sam, who had released the vampire but now had her sights set on the fae. "Bring it on, dog," Lucinda jeered.

There was nothing human about Sam as she dove for Lucinda with claws extended and canines out. The fae was ready, though, and sidestepped Sam. "Ah, ah, ah. I don't think so. You put one scratch on me and that's the end of you. No matter how much Finn wouldn't like it."

Lucinda taunted Sam, seeming to keep her distracted while magic flowed from Lucinda's wings. I thought the energy was going to enclose Sam, but instead, it formed a circle over the wolf's head and pulsed as if in sync with a heartbeat.

Sam's head flew back, and she screamed. As she did so, a black plume of fog shot out of her mouth and ricocheted around the circle Lucinda had created. "I've had my fair share of dark magic lately. I'm done with it," she sighed.

As soon as Sam's knees gave out and she dropped to the ground, Lucinda's hands moved in a circular motion. The barrier she'd made above Sam got smaller until it was nothing more than a six-inch orb.

"Unless one of you wants this as a souvenir, I'm going to give it back to the stone," Lucinda said.

Nobody objected, and the fae shoved the magic back where it belonged. At least, for now. Hopefully, someone would come along and destroy that thing sooner rather than later.

"Well, as entertaining as this has been, we have

better places to be." Lucinda met my stare as she grabbed on to Finn's arm. "Maybe I'll see you again."

"You guys should get out of here. I doubt the twelve witches you killed were the only ones here. More will be along. Be safe," Finn added right before the two of them dissipated into thin air.

Roman was already at Sam's side with Zeke hovering close by. The vampire's dark face was creased with concern, but I didn't sense any romance.

"Is she okay?" Zeke asked.

"No thanks to you," Roman spat as he gathered his cousin into his arms.

Sam coughed. "Zeke tried to stop me. Not his fault," she muttered.

Roman's grip on her tightened. "Next time she does something stupid, how about you come to her family for help instead of leaving her to suffer for days alone?"

Zeke's lip lifted in a snarl. "I did everything I could to help Samantha. Forgive me for not thinking you'd believe me if I went to you. By your warm welcoming, I can see how wrong I was to assume."

The vampire had a point, but I kept that thought to myself.

"Stop. Both of you." Sam coughed again until she choked. "What did that bitch do to me?"

"She saved your life. Try being more grateful. Oh, wait. That must not be a wolf thing," Zeke said.

I covered my mouth, hiding my grin. I would have thought meeting a vampire would scare the hell out of me, but damn, I had to admit I was finding a bit of enjoyment after all of the fighting.

The fight was something I was trying not to dwell on, because I was fairly certain I'd claimed the lives of a witch or two during the chaos. Just like Adira had said before, it was my life or theirs and I hadn't thought about my actions. I'd merely done whatever it took to survive.

Sam wiggled her way out of Roman's arms. "Roman, this is Zeke. I've run into him on occasion, and he's helped me a time or two."

"Or six," the vampire added.

"Anyway, I happened to see him on my way here, and he tried to talk me out of it. I didn't listen and got myself into some trouble. I would have been dead if it wasn't for him."

This didn't seem to make Roman feel any better. The alpha just glared at Zeke, who thought it would be appropriate to smile in return.

"Well, I don't know about the rest of you, but I'd like to take Lucinda's advice and get the hell out of here," Embry said, turning toward me. "Still have the portal spell?"

I patted my pockets. "Right here." Wonder laced my words that the vial hadn't broken during the fight. It must have been magically protected. From what I knew about Beatrix, I wouldn't have been surprised if so.

Roman reached his hand to Sam who hesitated to take it. She glanced up at Zeke. "Thank you for doing what you could."

He bowed. "Anything for you, Samantha."

I really wanted to know exactly how old the vampire was, but I kept my questions to myself, saving them for when I was alone with Embry later on.

The vampire nodded at the rest of us before blurring out of existence.

"You have some explaining to do, *Samantha,*" Roman said, and she rolled her eyes.

She shoved him out of the way and moved to stand between me and Embry. "Yeah, sure. Can we go home now?"

"I'm surrounded by too many women," Roman muttered before joining us.

Nobody else poked at him, all of us ready to be as far away from the bloodbath as possible.

17

CAIT

The sun was just rising when we got back to the pack, but I was nowhere near tired. Sam assured Roman she was fine and let him walk her up to her room after waving goodbye to Embry and me.

"Please tell me all of your adventures aren't that eventful," I said.

She smiled and looped her arm through mine. "Unfortunately not. Let's go get cleaned up and then you can ask the millions of questions I know you have."

I laughed. "You know me so well."

"I know you best."

We walked back to her house, and I let her shower first. Going to my room, I picked out new clothes for the day: loose tan, cotton shorts and a white tee. I wanted something comfortable, because I was hoping for lots of down time during the day.

Embry yelled at me when she got out of the shower, and I wasted no time getting in after her. I let the bathroom steam up and kept turning the water temperature up. Once it was as hot as I could handle, I let my head hang down as my body relaxed and closed my eyes.

My hope was to clear my head after everything that had happened, but instead, all I saw was blood and fangs and claws and dark magic as crimson and grime circled around the drain

I'd killed someone.

I was responsible for taking a life.

I'd been able to shove the act under the rug while I'd still been high on adrenaline, but that rush was gone, and reality slammed itself against my chest.

My breathing became rapid and tears fell from my eyes, getting lost in the stream of water until my cries turned into sobs. I understood I'd only done what I had to, and I'd repeat the same actions again if it came to that, but it didn't change the truth.

I was the reason someone wouldn't get up tomorrow.

That was heavy shit, no matter who you were or why it happened.

A knock sounded at the door, but I ignored Embry as I got my shit together. I'd allow this one breakdown, and then I needed to find a way to move on. Those witches had killed plenty of people, and I'd saved more lives than I probably wanted to know by ending theirs. I had to focus on that and nothing else.

The door cracked and groaned right before breaking

open. A very furious Roman stood in the small bathroom when I pulled the curtain back.

"What's wrong?" he demanded, chest heaving.

"Uh, the door is broken and you're letting cold air in here," I said, keeping myself covered with the shower curtain.

"You were crying," he stated, glancing around as if someone else might be hiding in the small bathroom.

"I've had a long day, or night, or whatever. I'm fine now." That was mostly the truth.

Let him heal you, Adira said.

There's nothing broken.

You haven't looked in the mirror, she quipped.

The wolf was right. I'd gone right into the shower without wanting to see any blood on my face or anywhere else. I held my finger up to Roman and closed the curtain before glancing down at myself. Sure enough, there were large bruises covering my left side, a deep scratch down my right arm, and something on the back of my thigh I couldn't really see without the risk of losing my balance in the shower.

I peeked my head out from the curtain again and gave him a pointed look. "I'll be out in a minute."

He looked around again, then nodded. "I'll be in your room."

Overprotective much? I thought as he turned to leave. Secretly, I loved that Roman cared so much. It was intense, but the more I was around him, the more his alpha tendencies grew on me.

"Shit," I muttered when I shut off the water. I'd left

my clothes on the bed. While I'd enjoyed the brief sexual encounter with Roman when I first got back, that had been an act of passion shared in a private space. Knowing Embry was around and after what we'd just done, the mood didn't scream "let's get naked" to me.

I went into my room, and Roman was sitting at the end of my bed with his back to me. I didn't say anything to him, and he didn't move as I reached for my clothes. My eyes stared at the back of his head, but there wasn't even the slightest flinch coming from him, so I let my towel drop a little and reached for my bra.

Getting dressed proved to be a little more challenging than I realized it would be, but I'd managed to get my bra and underwear on before I heard the bed creak and saw Roman standing.

"Let me help you." He was standing in front of me, meeting my stare, and I didn't have the will to object.

Roman reached for my shirt first and pushed it over my head. "I'm sorry you got hurt." His lips pressed against my collarbone as he gently moved my arms through the holes.

He knelt before me, leaning forward and kissing my stomach. "I should have known it was too quiet when we arrived."

My legs shook. "None of that was your fault."

His fingers wrapped around my calf, guiding my left foot into the shorts first as he stayed on the ground. Seeing him kneeling before me sucked the breath out of my chest. Roman was an alpha. He bowed to no one. Yet, he had no qualms about doing so for me.

How could I have ever thought I'd be able to walk away from him?

He gently moved my right foot into the shorts and worked the material up my legs. "Let me know if this hurts."

Oh, so much about it hurt, but not in the way he was thinking.

At the back of my thigh, where I hadn't been able to see well, I flinched as the cotton brushed over whatever wound was back there. "You should be healed by dinner. I had hoped for sooner given how quickly your ankle healed after the mill incident, but I think once you were able to release your power properly, it balanced some of your abilities out," he said as he stood, letting me button my own shorts.

"Expedited healing in any form is a definite perk to this wolf life," I said.

He stepped closer, his chest nearly touching mine. "I'm glad you think so. There are many more as well."

Exhaustion set in, even though my blood was pumping wildly at our close proximity. "I can't wait to learn about them all."

He used two fingers and lifted my chin. "Even after last night? You still want to stay?"

I grabbed hold of his shirt. "More than anything. I'm done running from my issues, Roman. I promise. I did it for years after my mom died, trying to regain some sort of control over my life, but I'd been doing it wrong. I need to face life's challenges. It's the only way I can live my best life."

He frowned. "I don't want you to face what's coming for you."

"We don't have a choice. Your grandfather is going to learn I'm alive, and I doubt he'll be happy about my escape."

Roman growled. "He's not my grandfather. Whatever hope there might have been between our families to one day put the past aside is long gone now. He and Kyle and that witch will pay for what they did to you even if it was what was meant to happen."

I rubbed my hand over his chest. "That's a problem for later. Let's at least have one day of quiet."

I'd gone from being kidnapped to becoming a wolf to a mini training session to a mission all in the last few days. I needed a break before we tackled any other problems. Most of all, I wanted Roman with me and not hunting his family down on his own.

His arms held me close, and I listened to his heart slow. "Do you want to stay here or come to the pack house with me?"

Roman had stayed with me here last time, and I was pretty sure his bed would be bigger, so I chose the pack house.

We left my room and found Embry laying on the couch. "Leaving so soon?"

"We're just going to the main house," Roman said.

Embry pouted and looked at me. "I'm going to lose my roommate, aren't I?"

"Uh…" I hadn't thought about living with Roman, even though I was sure it would be expected at some point, but Roman saved me before I could come up with an answer.

"Just today, or for however long she wants. I won't keep her if she doesn't want to stay," he said.

The only problem with his words was the thought of leaving him again. Now that I'd opened my heart, there was no closing it, but still, I appreciated that he respected my need to take things slow, regardless of how quickly my feelings were growing for him.

I leaned over the couch, hissing as I bent to give Embry a hug. "We'll have dinner, or a late lunch after we've both gotten some sleep?" I suggested.

"You know it, and I'm just giving you hell about spending time with him. Don't feel bad about your choices. I'm Team Cait. Whatever you want, I want for you. Bestie promise."

"I love you," I said and blew her a kiss from the door.

"I love you, too," she called back as Roman closed up behind us.

He peeked down at me. "I'd offer to carry you, but I don't want to hurt your leg."

"I wouldn't have let you anyway." I patted his arm with a grin.

Roman leaned in closer. "Are you trying to rack up more punishments? Don't think I haven't forgotten how you spoke to me before we left."

My steps faltered, and I heard a soft chuckle escape his lips. Oh, that bastard was good. Too good.

I'd find a way to get him back for whatever it was he

thought he had planned for me, but first, I wanted that nap I didn't think I'd need so soon.

I yawned, and he guided me up the porch stairs of the pack house. "Are you going to be able to make it up to my room?" he teased.

"I think I'll manage. Do you need a head start to hide anything?" I joked right back.

Tension rolled through him, and he stopped moving. I turned around. "What's wrong?"

"I have never brought a woman to my room or shared my bed with her. Not to say I haven't been with another, but my room is private, and I need you to know that this bed is only for myself and my mate." Roman reached a hand to me, stroking my cheek. "I would never disrespect you in such a way, even if I hadn't known you then."

Shit, he was too good to be true.

I leaned up onto my toes and pressed my lips to his. "I believe you."

He smiled down at me with a wicked glint in his eyes. Before I could ask what he was up to, he cradled my body to his chest, holding me up with one hand around my back and the other under my ass, careful to avoid the bruises.

"You walk too slow," Roman said while lengthening his stride. Before I knew it, we were entering the house and moving swiftly up the stairs that led to his room.

Once we made it to the top, he pushed open the door and kicked it closed behind us before setting me down. I faced the room, remembering I'd never been up there before.

In the center was a large king-sized, or bigger, bed with a forest-green comforter and three oversized pillows. To the left of that was a bay window and a padded bench I could see myself reading a book at. There was a small desk that appeared mostly unused. Two more doors were on the opposite wall of the window, likely leading to a closet and a bathroom.

With my perusal done, I eyed the bed once more, and another yawn escaped me. Roman pressed his hand against my lower back. "Come on. You need rest. Tomorrow, we're going to make you an official member of our pack."

"Is that all?" I asked, silently wondering how this whole mate thing worked.

"Yes, Cait. I would never trick you into anything more." His words clipped and I hadn't meant to offend him.

"I'm sorry. That's not what I meant. I just don't understand how," my hands waved between us, "this works."

"We're mates, but in order for us to be bonded, we have to willingly give ourselves to each other. Freely and without apprehension," he said.

"So, we just need to have sex?"

He laughed. "Essentially, but it's not guaranteed we'd bond even then if there is any hesitation by either mate."

Well, shit. That added a bit of pressure to the

situation. My libido went down a few degrees as I worried that I'd let my own head ruin what was supposed to be something meaningful.

"That's not for you to concern yourself with now. Today, we're just resting. Tomorrow, you're officially becoming part of a pack. Everything after that, we'll take one step at a time," Roman said as he urged me onto the bed.

Easy for him to say. He knew exactly what he wanted and wasn't afraid of it. At least he wasn't now.

While I was more accepting of so many things, there was a little piece of the old me that hadn't fully died. I needed to find a way to work through whatever reservations I had before I found myself in even more trouble than being kidnapped.

18

ROMAN

Sleep never came for me as I held Cait in my arms. In my attempt to keep her safe, I'd almost gotten myself killed. My decision to get Sam with just Embry and Cait had been idiotic at best. As soon as I'd gone through the illusion, the witches were waiting for me.

They'd known all along we were there and prepared for us the moment we thought we'd gotten away with our presence in Sydney. I should have known things couldn't be that easy.

My next step was to decide how far I wanted to take things. In order to get back at Cohen for initiating Cait's kidnapping, I had to tell the wolf council what he'd done. Unfortunately for me, my mother's sperm donor was a smart man. He'd know I would be leery about sharing details of how Cait came to be with anyone outside our pack.

From the sound of things, it was dumb luck Kyle had stumbled upon her and I now had tough decisions to make. Really there were three choices. One, I could tell the wolf leaders and hope they did their fucking job. Two, have Embry reach out to her parents and see who we could trust inside the supernatural council. Lastly, I could kill Cohen, Kyle, and the witch Callista myself, then run away with Cait.

The latter was the worst-case scenario, but not one I'd completely ruled out. I'd do anything to keep my mate safe and knew that Cohen, once he learned Cait was still alive, would find a way to come for her again.

Option three is my choice, my wolf said.

That's only because you're a selfish bastard.

Possibly, but it also keeps our mate safest.

I huffed. *And it might also make her hate us.*

To that, he had nothing to say, because I was right. If I took Cait away from all she'd begun to accept—away from Embry—I risked losing everything.

Hours after we had lay down, I still didn't want to leave my mate's side, but there were things that needed to be done, and I couldn't get anything accomplished lying in bed all day. I moved my pillow against Cait's side, and she snuggled into it, inhaling deeply.

I brushed her hair back, pleased she felt safe enough in my room to get solid rest. Once I was up, I wrote her a note and left it on the pillow in hopes it would be the first thing she found if I wasn't back by the time she woke.

Upon exiting my room, I found Sam leaning against the wall, paying more attention to her bitten-off nails than anything else.

"Samantha," I said with extra emphasis.

She flipped me off. "I lost a bet with the bloodsucker, and he managed to prove himself useful before I gutted him. Don't get your panties in a twist because I didn't tell you about him. He means nothing."

"But you trust him enough to help you with things you're not supposed to tell anyone else about?" I countered.

"I trust very few people, and you know that. Zeke? I tolerate him and believe he respects me enough not to fuck me over, but like I said, he means nothing to me. If anything happened to him, I could come home, and everything would still be okay." She tried to play nonchalant, but I read between the lines.

Putting Zeke in a precarious situation was his choice, but if she did the same to me, it would be her fault if things went sideways. Sam didn't show her emotions often, so I let the conversation go and shoved her down the hallway.

"It's okay, Sammy. I know you love me best. We don't need to get all mushy. How about you just tell me what the hell you were doing at that boulder?" I asked.

She groaned. "I wasn't supposed to be there. I was tracking a witch for the council. She was bouncing all over the place, and I'd lost her a couple times. I ran into Zeke, who said he knew of something big going down. Deciding a little back-up wasn't bad, I let him lead the way. The job was described as a simple grab and go, but nothing as of late has been how it's supposed to be."

I grunted. "I have to agree with that. So, you

showed up, there were too many of them, and you got pushed into the stone?"

"Something like that." Sam didn't like to talk about her jobs. She didn't brag about the things she had to do or the people she went after. Those were the only secrets she ever kept from me, and I never pressed her for more.

In this instance, I almost did for Cait's sake, but if there was something to do with my mate that Sam thought she'd stumbled upon, I trusted her to tell me on her own without me prying.

"I heard what's been happening. What are you doing about it?" she asked as we made our way down the stairs.

"I haven't decided yet. My gut tells me it's best to keep Cait a secret, but it seems more people already know about her than I'd like."

"Well, taking her out in public on a mission certainly didn't help," she said.

"She didn't give me much of a choice. Things are a bit fragile."

Sam laughed. "Is your she-wolf giving you a run for your money?"

I sighed—heavily—and ignored her question. Sam was only trying to get a rise out of me, and I wouldn't give her one.

She sobered. "Seriously, Ro. What are you going to do?"

"Just a minute," I said as we moved through the pack house. As soon as we were settled into the privacy of my office, I explained the options I'd come up with.

For several minutes after, she stayed quiet, staring at my window before finally turning toward me. "She's really that powerful?" I nodded. "Then, you need to run."

"Excuse me?" I couldn't believe she'd gone with that choice.

"Things aren't as they should be, as you've been learning and as I've said already. Cait is only one piece to the balance. Beatrix and the Moon Goddess were right to interfere. I just didn't know it was getting so out of hand this quickly."

I took two paces toward Sam and grabbed her shoulders. "What the hell are you talking about?"

"I've been trying to find an out from my work with the council. I tried reaching out to Embry's parents for help, but they're deep underground somewhere. The missions I've been sent on lately aren't what they're supposed to be. The witch I followed to Sydney wasn't the first mishap I've had."

Mother hell. "Are you saying we're on our own here and there is nobody we can trust outside this pack?"

She shrugged. "It's a possibility. More of a gut feeling based on what I've been seeing lately. I planned to tell you about what I thought when I got home. I didn't expect you to have to get so involved."

Sam was a smart woman. One of the best I knew. I knew she'd only keep things to herself to avoid causing trouble where there was none. I wished she was wrong, but with the things we'd found out lately, I knew she wasn't.

"We'll figure it out. We always do. For now, running isn't an option. When the time is right, I'm going to feel out the wolf council myself and see where they stand and what they know. Now that I'm aware things might not be as they seem, it will be easier to look for what they're trying to hide."

"There's five of them and one of you. What if they don't like what you have to say?" she asked.

"They won't touch me without just cause and risk ruining their precious reputation. If they want me gone, they'll provoke me without getting their hands dirty and hope for the best."

She leaned back against the window. "And if they push too far and win? What then?"

"Option three is always there. I know how to disappear if needed."

"What about your mate? Can she handle all of this? From what I've heard, she's a bit more unprepared than is helpful," Sam added.

"Cait did well in Sydney. I was close to being stuck in that rock alongside you and she got me out. She just needs to learn more. It's only been a handful of weeks since she learned the supernatural world even existed." From what I had seen so far, Cait was a fast learner and eager to be in control of what was inside her. Even though I didn't like it, she was going to be our biggest advantage once we learned what she could really do.

"I hope you'll have enough time," Sam said before

standing back up. "I haven't slept yet. Too much adrenaline. I'm going to go for a run and use up the last of my energy before crashing. I'll see you tomorrow?"

I moved into her path and gave her a hug. "I'm glad you're home."

She nodded against my chest. "Me, too."

Once she left my office, I sat down to figure out the best way to train Cait without drawing attention or overwhelming her. Before I could make one note, Vaughn knocked on the door.

"Come on in," I said.

Even through his beard, I could see a grim expression on his face. "Why didn't you come back for me when things weren't what they seemed?"

"I thought we had a handle on it. The witches had an illusion shield over the boulder holding all of the souls and magic. We didn't know until it was too late."

"Yeah, well, I don't want your job so maybe try to stay alive for a while longer until that mate of yours starts popping out alpha pups. That'd be great," he grumbled.

I laughed. "I'm sorry my unexpected death would have been inconvenient for you. How selfish of me not to consider all involved."

He nodded stiffly. "I'm glad you see reason. Now, what the hell are we going to do about what's happening?"

"Did anything new come up while I was gone?" I asked.

"No, but tensions are high. You've been gone a lot,

and the pack is starting to get worried it's not going to be safe here much longer. A few have already left to the cabin areas we have further up north."

As much as I didn't like our pack separating, it wasn't the worst idea to have people spread out more. "Send a couple of your guys to keep watch over the families that left. If there are any other groups of people who want to leave, offer the same to them. We won't keep anyone where they don't want to be."

"I already sent Rich and Nita up. I'll be sure to see if there are any other volunteers in case we need them," Vaughn replied, and I should have known he'd already be on it.

He wasn't born an alpha, so he could never respectfully take over my position, but he did a damn good job at it when I was otherwise occupied.

Another knock sounded and my dad came in. "Your mate woke up, and Mom found her first."

"Are you saying she'll be busy for the foreseeable future, then?" I asked with a grin.

Dad nodded. "Likely, yes. You'll probably find them at Embry's house or the training field. From the sounds of it, Cait wasn't wanting to stay idle today."

Of course she wasn't. How could I have ever thought she would be vulnerable as my mate? Cait was so much stronger than I ever could have expected.

"Then, let's get to business," I said as my dad joined Vaughn in taking a seat.

It was time to prepare for whatever was coming for us.

19

CAIT

Waking up in a new room after the craziness of the day before left me out of sorts until I stretched and found Roman's note. He'd kept it short but sweet, telling me his bed had never been more comfortable before, but unfortunately, he had work to do.

After getting out of the blankets I'd cocooned myself into, I headed for the bathroom. I opened the wrong door and found a walk-in closet. Everything was color-coordinated and placed perfectly in its own space. Not a sleeve or seam was out of place.

"Oh, someone has a bit of OCD when it comes to their stuff," I said with enjoyment. Stepping into the closet, I pushed a few of the shirts further apart than they'd been before and nudged a couple of his shoes out of place. "That's better."

I went to the last door, hoping to find the toilet, and almost died of happiness. Roman had been hiding a bathroom fit for the royals up here and he was going to know how jealous I was. There was a deep clawfoot tub to my right and a tile shower just beyond that with three showerheads.

A double sink with a sit-down vanity in the middle took up the left side of the bathroom, and another door leading to the toilet was at the back. I wasn't sure how I'd missed that he was so clean and tidy, but the more I saw, the hotter it became. I was half-tempted to go put his closet back how I'd found it, but messing with him on occasion couldn't be passed up.

My fingers trailed over the smooth granite counters as I padded along the warm tile floor. Wait, warm? The tiles were heated, and I was officially moving into the bathroom.

Even the toilet was pristine, and I wondered if he cleaned everything himself or if one of the other wolves in his pack came by to take care of the task for him. I preferred the former.

I took care of business, then washed up at the sink as best I could. I'd probably only been asleep a few hours based on how low the sun still was, but I didn't want to come out of Roman's room looking like a hot mess, either.

Opening the drawers, I found one with a new toothbrush, hairbrush, and other random products I usually kept on hand. "Roman Chase, you're a total stalker," I snickered as I grabbed the items I wanted.

I tamed my long locks and brushed my teeth before leaving the bathroom. With one last glance at the tub, I made promises to the inanimate object that I would be back. Vaughn wasn't so crazy after all being in a relationship with his motorcycle Susy.

After making the bed as well as I could, I took one last look around the room to make sure I hadn't left a mess for Roman to find. Everything seemed in place, so I headed out the door. Roman's room was the only one in this part of the house, so it was easy to find the stairs and head back down.

My intention had been to go to his office and let him know I was up, but I crossed paths with Ramona first.

She threw her arms around me as soon as she saw me. "Oh, Cait! I'm so glad I saw you."

"I can tell." I laughed, and she loosened her hold a bit.

"Sorry. It's been a stressful week. I needed a moment to make sure you were okay," she said sheepishly. It was the first time I'd seen her anything other than confident.

"The hug was appreciated. I promise." I hadn't had one like that since my mom was alive, and I'd forgotten how safe a mother's hug could feel.

"Are you doing anything before tonight?" she asked.

"Tonight?"

Her eyes narrowed. "Did my son forget to tell you about the pack ceremony?"

"Oh, that. No, he didn't. I just forgot for a moment. He's mentioned it a few times actually."

"Good. So, do you have any plans today?"

I shrugged. "I was going to go see Roman to let him know I was up and then head to Embry's. Nothing special."

She nodded. "Jack will tell Roman you're up and with me. What do you need at Embry's?"

I laughed. "I don't *need* anything, but it sounds like you do. I'm all yours."

"I'm just excited that you're staying. I know things aren't settled completely yet, but having you here means so much to a lot of us," she said, giving my hand a squeeze before guiding us toward the front door.

"Really? I had the impression that most of the people here would rather I'd leave."

Ramona waved a hand in the air. "Not at all. Maybe at first, but you're one of us. There isn't a person here who wouldn't fight for your safety."

Interesting. I wasn't sure I believed her, but I was glad she thought so.

"Where are we headed?" I asked as we started across the yard, in the opposite direction of Embry's cabin.

"There are some things I've been wanting to try since you came back. Things Roman might not approve of without proof they won't hurt you, so…"

"So, we need to be quick and discreet before we get caught?" I finished with a grin.

"Exactly. As long as you don't mind."

"Not at all, as long as you don't mind answering some questions I've had since we got back this morning," I replied.

Embry had gone over a lot about the supernatural world, but my curious mind never seemed to shut off and there were a few things I couldn't let go of.

"Of course not. What's on your mind?" she asked as we headed for the tree line. Their land was flat as the desert, but still managed to be full of lush grass and trees. I imagined they had the humidity to thank for that. At least that devil was good for something.

"I know the Moon Goddess created wolves, but what about the others? Vampires, witches, fae?" I asked. After meeting them and seeing how human they seemed, I couldn't help but wonder if they were all born like me and then turned into something else at some point.

"That's a great question given what you've been through. Witches were the first supernatural. Though, some fae will argue they were first and just stayed hidden away. Witches are the most human of us all. From my understanding, the original witch was born from human parents, but had the ability to acquire energy. As she grew older, she explored her talents and harnessed the Earth's natural magic, then sought others like her to teach them what they were capable of.

"As far as fae go, we have no clue how they came to be. For all anyone knows, they could be aliens." Ramona and I shared a laugh before she continued. "They have their own realm out in the middle of the Indian Ocean. As long as they don't cause trouble, none of the rest seem to mind what they choose to do."

"Lucinda seems like the kind to cause trouble," I said.

Ramona grinned. "She stayed on Earth for an extended period of time and did just that, but deep down, she was actually helping, even when she acted as if she didn't care about anyone other than herself."

I could see that after meeting the fae. She could have easily walked away from us back in Sydney, but she and Finn had stuck around. Without them, I was almost certain we would not have gotten Sam out on our own.

"And vampires?" I asked. Too much had been going on for me to concern myself with Zeke the night before, but I wondered how often they killed people to survive and how many of those deaths were human or supernatural.

Ramona paused, leaning against a tree. "That's a bit more complicated. Vampires came last. Some say they're a creation of a demon, but most of them are made by being bitten. Every vampire, no matter how they're made, can create more once they have a control over their thirst. There was an original family: the father a vampire and the mother a human."

I choked on my laugh as the scenario reminded me of my first vampire read. "So, he turned her, and they had babies? Wait, can they have kids after they're a vampire?"

"No, the night demons can't have children like the rest of us do. Their families are usually created, but for the original vampire? His queen remained human and gave birth to ten sons and one daughter—all who were born vampire and stopped aging in their early twenties."

Holy shit. I was intrigued beyond anything. I wanted to know more about the hierarchy, how long they lived, and if that differed for those born versus those made into vampires. So many questions about creatures I had no desire to actually spend any time with.

As I thought of the most important questions to ask, Ramona smiled at me, a bit of sinister peeking through her eyes. "Watch where you stand, Cait," she warned.

I turned my head in all directions to see what she was up to. *You sense anything, Wolfie?*

That's not my name, she hissed.

It has a better ring to it than Adira. Not that Adira is a ba—shit!

Something tore into my shoulder. "What the hell was that?" I screeched.

"Plastic bullets. Hurts a little, doesn't it?" Ramona said calmly.

Another landed in my thigh. "Are you trying to kill me?" I asked as I moved to stand further behind a tree.

"No. We're making you stronger," she replied.

Two more shots landed as she spoke: one in my shoulder and the other in my calf. Mother hell, Embry and Serene must have been helping her.

A little help would be appreciated, I said to Adira.

You're on your own for this one. I'm tired, was my wolf's only reply, no matter how many times I yelled at her.

I growled at Ramona as a sixth bullet hit me. None of them were breaking my skin, but they stung like a bitch and were leaving deep purple bruises wherever they hit.

I gathered my energy and created the barrier around myself, making it bigger until Ramona was forced to back up or risk getting singed by the heat.

"I'd start moving if I was you," Ramona said.

"I don't like you," I snapped as I started to move away.

She laughed. "I'll be your mother-in-law soon. You're not supposed to like me."

I rolled my eyes and kept moving. I needed to find where Embry and Serene were hiding, so I could take them out before I looked more like a dalmatian than human.

My breathing slowed once I was away from Ramona and not out in the open as much. I listened carefully, noticing Adira's interest rise in whatever game I'd found myself in.

A twig snapped somewhere to my right, and I heard an intake of breath. The ground was littered with leaves that would give me away, so I chose another option.

Jumping up, I grabbed on to a tree branch, swinging my body back and forth until I had enough momentum to get up. From there, I leaped between the trees, using the barren branches to keep my movements quiet.

Serene was below me, and she had no idea I'd found her. The old bitty was crouched on the ground, gun up and searching for me. A part of me felt guilty about what I planned to do next given her age, but she fired shots first.

With a slight shove, I descended toward the ground and landed on top of her, a purple hue still glowing around me, but no longer hot.

She rolled over underneath me, and her eyes widened. "What the hell happened to your face?"

"No need to be rude just because you lost," I said, pressing down on her.

She shook her head. "Seriously. Your face. Look at your hands. They're the same way."

One quick peek was all I allowed myself in case she was playing me. Except that "quick peek" turned into a minute-long stare with my mouth hanging open.

My skin was translucent, like a damned ghost. "What happened to me?"

"That's what I said." Serene huffed and pushed me off of her, leaving her gun leaning against the tree.

Ramona and Embry arrived at the same time and lost their grins immediately. "Whoa, freaky," Embry said, moving her hand over my arm, then pulled out her phone and took a picture. "You still show up, so you're not dead," she added.

"Not helpful, Em," I droned.

Adira? I called.

You're in spirit form.

What the hell does that mean?

That you can't be hurt and you're untraceable.

I sighed. *You didn't think that would be helpful when we were in Sydney?*

I didn't know you could do that then.

Oh, that wolf was something else.

"Makes sense considering you're Luna Marked. There had to be something more about you than the friction energy you put off. We just had to draw it out," Ramona said after I passed along Adira's thoughts.

"Why wouldn't this particular perk have come out when we nearly died yesterday?" I asked.

"Probably because you were more concerned with Roman than yourself. Today you were the only one in danger, and now that you're not… you're back to normal."

I lifted my arms and sure enough my skin, while still bruised, was back to its normal coloring. "Am I supposed to say thank you for trying to kill me? Or maybe you were just trying to scare me away."

Embry laughed and hip-checked me. "Oh, what fun would that be? Without you here to bring the drama, we'd be bored out of our minds."

I glared at her. "Not funny."

"Someone has to keep humor." She shrugged.

"So, was that it? Are you done with me now?" I asked the three of them.

Serene cackled. "Not even close. Now, you need to learn to do all the things you're capable of on demand. The men around here don't always like to show us women how to do the heavy lifting, because then it makes them feel less useful. We're here to make sure you can keep yourself safe."

I wasn't sure she was entirely accurate. Roman

seemed perfectly fine with me learning how to use whatever magic I was gifted with, but I went with it because, regardless of their reasoning, I needed to be more prepared.

"Alright. Let's get to it, then," I said.

As I met each of their grins, I knew they were about to have a hell of lot more fun than I was.

20

CAIT

Not only did I look like the dead, but I also felt like it.

Hours of torture passed, and the only part of my body not bruised and battered was my face. Embry and Ramona had the time of their lives putting mine in dangerous situations until I found my triggers.

After three hours, I was finally able to draw on my spirit form without needing fear to draw it out, and I could shift while all ghost-like, which made me even more of an oddity, even by supernatural standards.

"You did really well today, Cait. I knew you were going to be strong the moment I met you," Ramona said as we walked back. Well, they walked, and I hobbled to keep up.

"I'm glad the torment was all worth it, then," I deadpanned, and each of them laughed.

"I need to go hide my wrinkles for the ceremony. See

you children later," Serene said as she shifted to wolf form and bounded through the trees.

"She really is odd," I said.

"But she cares a lot. You should have seen her after you were taken. She was nearly as enraged as Roman was," Ramona said.

"No, I was second in line for that. Serene can have third," Embry added.

"At least everything worked out how it was supposed to," I said, trying to lighten the situation.

Ramona nodded. "That it did. So far anyway, but one thing at a time. Now, we have to sneak you past the pack house without Roman catching sight of you."

I pointed to the bruises all over me. "These are going to be pretty hard to hide."

Embry grinned. "We left your face alone for a reason. We can keep the marks hidden until after you've officially become a pack member."

"How?" I asked.

"You get to wear an outfit passed down from generations of shifters. Every new pack member not born here has worn it," Ramona said.

My face scrunched. "What is it?"

"A dress with lots of ruffles." Embry's grin was wide, and I knew I was in for lots of pictures.

Ramona shoved her. "It's not a dress."

"It doesn't have legs and goes past the knees. That makes the fabric a dress," Embry said.

"Call it what you want, but there's nothing embarrassing about it. Like I said, many before you have worn it. Even myself. It will hide all of the evidence of today's adventures. You just need to quit wincing every time you step with your left leg."

Oh, was that all? They weren't the one beaten to hell. Regardless, I was excited for the ceremony, and I could sense the rising interest of Adira as the time got closer. She'd been quiet, but something told me that being part of a pack meant more to her than I was capable of understanding yet.

I got brief thoughts from her that included family, pack, safety, and home. Maybe one day she would feel comfortable enough to tell me about her past lives. My main hope was that not all of them were bad and that she hadn't been too lonely without a mate.

We arrived near the pack house and went around the back, taking the long way to Embry's house. "Will we wait at your house until it's time?" I asked her.

"You know, you live there, too. It's just as much mine as it is yours for however long you want it to be," she replied with a wink.

"I appreciate that. I haven't really thought of anywhere as home since I left Oregon," I admitted.

Ramona wrapped an arm around me. "We can never replace the family you lost, but I hope you'll see us as such and feel at home in time. We already consider you one of us."

Flutters grew in my stomach, warming my heart. "Thank you, Ramona. It means more to me than you know."

"Our upbringing wasn't the same, but I found my place here, so I understand on some level."

I nodded, not wanting to imagine growing up with Cohen as a father. He was evil, through and through.

"Was Kyle always the way he is now?" I asked.

Ramona frowned. "No. At least I don't think so. I wasn't close with him since I'd left the pack before he was born, but his mother, my sister-in-law, had a heart of gold. I used to pray he'd take after her. Unfortunately, my father got to him at some point, and it seems Kyle never looked back."

"There was nothing you could have done, Ramona. He made his choices," Embry replied, and something told me they'd had this conversation before.

"Come on. Let's get ready. We only have another hour before we need to be back at the pack house," Ramona said, pasting on a smile and pushing down the past.

I hoped I could be just as strong as her after some more time in the pack. She was a wolf to be admired.

///

FORTY-FIVE MINUTES LATER, I WAS WEARING A HIDEOUS brown gown that had ruffles around the neck and down the arms before falling over my legs, even less flattering than a pillowcase would have been.

"Whoever created this dress hated who it was intended for," I grumbled.

"On the plus side, you're no longer wincing, and

nobody can see your battle scars. Plus, your hair is on point. Just smile bright and nobody will even see the dress," Embry said as she shoved another bobby pin in the crown braid she'd made out of my hair.

"Thank you both for believing in me and helping today. I wouldn't be as sure of what came next without your support," I said, reaching out to both of them.

Even though Ramona was the mother of a man I almost rejected completely, she'd never judged me for my choices. She'd only supported and guided me to the best of her ability. As for Embry, she was my favorite asshole in this world. She had a mouth on her and said things at all the wrong times, but she was my best friend.

Ramona's eyes glistened as she cleared her throat. "I'm going to head over now. I'll meet you guys out back soon?"

"You got it," Embry replied.

As soon as we were alone, I started to laugh as my thoughts got distracted. "What's so funny?" Embry asked.

"Well, I was just thinking about how you're such an asshole, but how much I love you for being just who you are. I've come up with a new name for you."

She raised a brow. "Oh, yeah? What's that?"

"Asstie." I grinned wide.

Embry stared at me with a blank face for all of two seconds before she laughed so hard that spit flew from her mouth, and she started snort-giggling. "I have no idea how your insane brain came up with that, but I freaking love it. Nearly as much as I love you. Asshole and bestie have never sounded so good together."

She hugged me tight, and we giggled like schoolgirls while calling each other asstie. Yeah, that one was going to stick for years to come.

"Come on, Asstie. It's time to go. Night is almost here," Embry announced once we regained control of ourselves.

I nodded and took a deep breath. I was ready for this. There was no hesitation. I'd truly accepted my old life was gone and I was part of this new, crazy, and moderately scary supernatural one. If I was going to survive, embracing all the things was the only answer.

I lifted the dress, so I didn't trip while walking through the trees and grinned at my converse. At least I'd gotten to pick my own shoes.

"Holy hell, it's hot as Hades out here," I complained as the dress seemed to stick to my skin, even though the sun was already beginning its descent.

"Don't worry. It won't take long, and you can take the robe-dress off," Embry said, ushering me along the path.

With a heavy sigh, I ignored the uncomfortableness and walked at a pace that didn't make me sweat more than I already was.

"When does the heat go away?" I asked when we got to the backyard.

Embry laughed. "Uh, a couple months out of the year it's quite pleasant around here."

"Just a couple? Great."

Roman was waiting outside already. He was standing in front of rows and rows of benches, and behind him was a white arch covered in dead vines that somehow fit perfectly with the setting. Except Adira threw an image of Roman in a tuxedo through my mind, causing me to stumble.

I was not ready for a wedding. Not a chance in hell.

I could sense her contentment at screwing with me. I needed to stop calling her Wolfie and pissing her off, but sometimes it just rolled off the tongue.

Embry nudged me forward as Roman's face creased with concern. I got my emotions in check, knowing that he wasn't rushing me into anything I wasn't ready for. This wasn't a wedding. It was a ceremony to tie me to the pack, not him.

As we came up on his left, Serene was headed over from the opposite direction. She grinned widely and stared at me. "Ready to promise yourself to the alpha?"

My eyes widened. "Excuse me?"

"Yeah, to be part of a pack, you need to be tied to the alpha. It's how he attempts to keep us all in line."

Okay, maybe this was more like a wedding than I'd been led to believe. I glanced at Roman, who was glaring daggers at Serene. "Enough." Then, he turned to me. "What she means to say is you will pledge your loyalty to me as your alpha and nothing more. Every member here has done the same, and I promise it does nothing more than link you to all of us so we can be stronger together as a pack."

Embry nodded. "Even though I was born here,

when I was ten, I pledged my allegiance to Jack and then it was transferred to Roman when he took over."

Not a wedding. Not a wedding. Not a wedding.

"Great," I said with a bit too high of a pitch and forced a smile to my face.

Roman sighed and pulled Serene aside. I couldn't hear what he said to her as they walked away, but I was happy with the moment of space. I would not freak out. I wanted to do this. I wanted to be part of the pack and have a home where I could feel safe and loved. All of the things Adira wanted, I did, too.

Roman came back, but Serene did not, and the other pack members started to fill the benches. I focused on the new arrivals, most of whom I didn't know, but a decent amount I was beginning to recognize. At some point, when things weren't so hectic, I was going to need to learn all of their names.

"I'm going to take a seat in the front row. It's going to be just you and Roman up there, but I'll be right here cheering you on," Embry said, giving me a hug.

"Thank you," I replied.

"Anything for you, Asstie." She winked, and I let the last of my nerves go as I tried not to laugh all over again at the nickname.

Roman raised a brow. "Asstie?"

"Would you rather her call me Kitten?" I challenged.

He leaned in, breath hot against my already warm skin. "That is reserved just for me and in private." The rumble in his voice had my muscles tightening. We needed some more private time that didn't include napping.

His lips skimmed over my cheek as he pulled back. "After."

Jesus, I was never going to survive the feelings he pulled from me.

Roman cleared his throat and raised his voice. "Thank you everyone for joining us today. I know you all have a lot of questions and Vaughn has been doing his best to keep everyone informed, but I hope today will help you see that what has been happening here is important for all of us."

Smiles and nods were on the faces of most of the people in the crowd.

"Cait wasn't born like us, but she was chosen by our creator and gifted with an incredible wolf spirit. She is powerful and capable and is going to be an asset to our pack." Roman met my stare and smiled. "She is also my mate, and, while she is not the official alpha female of the pack yet, she will be treated as such."

I expected at least one objection, but there was none, and I felt no discontentment thrown my way, either. Maybe things really had changed.

"Today we welcome Cait into our pack, as part of our family. Until further notice, I still ask that you keep her presence here to yourselves. I won't lie to you and tell you that everything is going to be easy moving forward. We all know that power often brings the unwanted. I will do my best to keep trouble away from the pack, but you need to know it's possible that some of it will land on our doorstep."

Murmurs began in hushed tones, but still, nobody was angry, and I didn't understand why. I certainly would have been.

Pack means family. You are one of them, or you will be soon. They will protect you no matter the risk, Adira said, reminding me of Ramona's earlier words.

If I was going to officially become a wolf, I needed to get better at thinking like one. She was right. I had to stop stressing so much about the things I had no control over.

Roman gave my hand a squeeze and continued, "But that's not why we're here today. I know it's hot out, so I'll proceed." He turned to face me, our shoulders square with each other. "Do you, Cait Jones, accept me, Roman Chase, as your alpha and the East Texas pack as your family?"

"I accept," I said without hesitation.

"Do you promise to protect our lands and the wolves who live here without apprehension?"

"I promise."

Roman grabbed on to my right hand and pulled out a small blade from his pocket with his other hand. I tried to jerk mine away, but he was ready and didn't let me go. Oh, I was going to hurt all of them for not telling me about whatever was happening next.

Roman spoke, sure and proud. "I vow to bleed for you, to protect you, and do what is best for this pack in exchange for your acceptance as a member of our family. Here, you will always be safe and always have a place to call home."

My heart warmed, and I forgot all about the dagger in his free hand. Tears filled my eyes as emotions got the best of me. I hadn't expected for his words to touch me so deeply. It was more than I imagined in all the best ways.

Tingles ran along my skin as I took slow breaths, soaking in the exchange. I had no idea what was happening, but I knew there was something unseen moving between us.

I tilted my head back, closing my eyes, and soaked up whatever Roman was sharing with me. As I was entranced with magic at work, there was a prick on my fingertip, but I paid the sensation no attention, trusting Roman was doing whatever he needed to complete the ceremony.

Pressure increased on my hand, then moved through my arm until it landed in my chest. Power swirled inside me, stronger than ever before until I felt like I was floating. Everything around me was light and pure and intense.

Finally, I opened my eyes to search for Roman. He was standing before me, basking in a hue of purple. We were still connected, and the barrier I'd created without meaning to cover us both. His jaw was clenched, and his eyes were bright, yet he said nothing to me while everyone around us was silent.

What the hell have I done?

21

ROMAN

Whatever energy Cait transferred to me was unlike anything I'd ever experienced. As alpha, I shared a connection with each of my pack members, but I hadn't thought what it would mean to share that same link with Cait.

If I hadn't been certain that she was special before, there was no denying it now. My body vibrated with power, tearing through me so furiously that I thought I'd be forced to shift.

She is the most perfect specimen I've ever seen, my wolf murmured as we fought to keep control.

I wanted to agree with him, but I was afraid if both of us got distracted, the pack would see us collapse under the pressure of whatever was happening.

What the hell have I done?

Cait's voice sounded in my mind, and my eyes widened.

Cait?

She tensed and nodded. *You can hear me?*

It doesn't normally happen that fast, but yes, I can.

How do I make this stop? she asked.

Just take a deep breath. Grab control of your power and call it back to you.

I saw the rise and fall of her chest as she slowly drew in breaths. While she was concentrating, I kept my eyes on her, watching as the barrier around us dimmed. She was doing it, and I was damn proud of her.

After a solid minute, the tension pulling at me loosened and I was able to relax and turn toward the pack. Everyone was staring and leaning forward in their seats. Vaughn, Embry, and my parents were surrounding us, stress creasing their faces.

I forced a smile. "Everything is fine. Like I said, Cait is special. We don't know the lengths of her abilities, but I assure you, they are not a threat to any of us."

Shifters began to stand. Once everyone was on their feet, they kneeled to the ground, bowing their heads in a show of respect that Cait deserved.

I grabbed her hand, bringing her close. "This is the pack formally welcoming you."

She held her head high and stepped forward. "Thank you everyone for trusting me. I promise not to let you down."

I hadn't expected her to speak, and while her words were simple, I knew the pack would appreciate them.

"We will see you all this weekend for the pack dinner. Thank you again for coming," I said before we walked back toward the pack house.

The crowd stepped aside as we passed, bowing their heads once again. It wasn't often they were so formal, but the ceremony was a ritual to be cherished, and I appreciated how seriously they took the process.

Once we were inside, I led Cait up to my room with Embry and Vaughn right on our heels. Nobody said anything until we were upstairs and behind closed doors.

"What the hell was that?" Vaughn asked first.

All eyes went to Cait. "I have no idea. It's not like I've done that before."

"I think that when I mixed our blood to finalize the ceremony, I took on more than just her normal wolf power. I received some of her Luna Marked ability," I said.

Cait's brows furrowed in confusion, so I continued. "As alpha, I draw power from the strongest of our pack and share my strength with the rest of them. It's a revolving circle of magic that ebbs and flows as needed. For instance, when you were sick and I helped speed up your healing process without realizing, the pack felt the draw on my energy."

"So, we now share the same magic?" she asked.

"I don't think it's the same, but I received a boost like nothing I've ever experienced before."

Vaughn eyed me, his lips turning into a pout that didn't suit him. "You do seem a little taller."

While I didn't want to give him any more reason to whine, I had to agree that my clothes seemed tighter than before.

"Regardless, I think this is a good thing. Cait got control of her magic, and I'm fine. The rest of it we'll sort out tomorrow," I said.

"Are you kicking us out so you can have 'alone time'?" Vaughn used his fingers to create air quotes.

I shoved him back toward the door. "Actually, yes."

Embry stayed put. "Are you okay with this?"

I didn't turn around. I didn't want to put pressure on Cait, but something told me she needed the connection of our bond just as much as I did.

"I am." Her words were sure, and I breathed a sigh of relief.

Vaughn waggled his brows at me. "Enjoy!"

"Out. Now."

Before I could give him another push in the right direction, Embry did the job for me. She waved goodbye with her back to us, and I closed the door. When I turned around, Cait's heated gaze was on me.

"That was..."

"A lot," I finished her sentence.

"To put it mildly. I know you've never had anything like that happen before, but was the process at all similar to other members you've added to the pack?" she asked.

With three long strides, I closed the gap between us, pressing one hand over her heart and the other behind her head so she was trapped in place. "There is nothing, and I mean *nothing,* similar about what we share in comparison to anyone else."

A slow smile spread across her face, and I kissed it

off her lips, sucking in the gasp she let out when I shocked her. Backing her up, I only slowed when I felt her legs hit the bed. My room wasn't as private as the cabin, but I didn't plan on luring her into sex. I just needed to feel my mate.

My hand trailed down her spine until I gripped her ass and pressed her closer. "I won't let things get too far. We will take the evening slowly, even if in the moment you think you want more. I won't let you regret what happens between us."

Her eyes glistened under the glow of my bedroom light as she nodded. "I trust you."

My hands squeezed her ass, then crept back up, caressing every inch of her until I felt the knots in her shoulders. The pads of my thumbs worked on the tense spots as I placed several kisses along her jawline. My mate had been working hard to gain control over the changes thrown at her, and I planned to show her how much I appreciated her efforts.

My lips moved along her collarbone, down her chest, and back up again until I nipped at her plump lips. "Wait right here."

She let out a small huff that made me grin. "I promise it will be worth it."

I turned around, and she smacked my ass. "It better be. Also, you're in trouble for not telling me about that epic bathroom of yours before."

Without thinking, I spun back toward Cait and hauled her over my shoulder. "Never mind. You're coming with me."

She squealed and acted like she was trying to get away, but there was no real effort to escape. My fingers splayed over her ass and gave it a good spank. "Whatever you do to me, I will do back. Just remember that, Kitten. And we still have your punishments to consider."

Cait's movements paused, and I sensed her arousal. I had my mate right where I wanted her. Depositing her on the counter, I turned toward the tub and began to fill it up. Moving back to Cait, her scent called me in a way nothing ever had before.

My fingers itched to tear her clothes apart and devour every inch of her, but that wasn't the way to my mate's heart. No, she needed tender love, even if she didn't know it, and I planned to give her everything I had and then some.

She was still in the god-awful ceremony gown, and yet, I'd never wanted her more. I peeled the layers back and snarled when I saw her arms. "What happened?"

"Just a bit of practice. I'm fine," she said, still breathing heavily.

I wanted to question her about what sort of training dotted her precious skin in bruises, but that wasn't on the agenda for the night and not what she needed.

Instead, I placed kisses over every mark, including the crescent-moon shape—which had turned obsidian in color—as I pushed the gown off her shoulders and pulled her arms out of it. She was wearing the same outfit as earlier, and her skin glowed against the light-colored clothing.

"You're absolutely stunning," I whispered against her stomach as I kneeled before her, something I often found myself doing with her. I wanted Cait to know I held her above all, myself included.

Cait's hands dug into my hair, gripping tightly as I inched her tank top up. The last, and really only, time we'd been together like this, everything had been frenzied, but I was in no hurry now. Nobody was waiting for us, and we had all night.

Her shirt went over her head and as her lips reappeared, I captured them with my own. She moaned beneath my movements as I jerked her closer. Cait's nails scratched down my back, and her legs wrapped around my waist, but I wasn't done with her yet. No, we were only getting started.

Pushing her back, I unclipped her bra with one hand and worked on her shorts with the other, going slowly in case she wanted to stop me. Instead of that, her hands worked on my pants with jerky movements that made the process take longer than it should have, but I let her handle that as I started pulling pins from her hair.

As my pants began to slip down, I yanked her off the counter and grinned down at her when she was left in nothing but her white cotton underwear. "Pure perfection. I'm the luckiest man alive."

"I'd say we're both pretty lucky," she replied, slipping her hands under my shirt as I kicked my jeans the rest of the way off.

I hesitated to get her completely naked, but she took

one look at the almost full tub and finished undressing herself before sidestepping me and getting in. "Are you joining me, or did you fill this ginormous thing just for me?"

My boxers were on the floor before she could finish her sentence, and I watched her eyes while she took all of me in. Pleased Cait couldn't manage to meet my eyes, I stepped into the water and leaned over her, lifting her chin up. "All of me is yours."

I kissed her before she had a chance to respond. My words weren't meant to get anything out of her. I just needed Cait to know that she was my life now. There was nothing, not even the pack, that meant more to me than her. Everything that I was, everything that I would be, belonged to Cait.

She clung to me as I devoured her mouth, using one hand to angle her head and the other to grasp her delectable ass I couldn't seem to get enough of.

While I'd gotten most, if not all, of the pins from her hair, it was still knotted in a braid. My fingers began to unravel the strands so she could fully wash up. When I was done, I realized the position we were in was too much too soon if I had any hope of keeping control.

Cait's legs straddled me, and my dick pressed against her stomach, twitching with need. "Turn around," I said, voice deeper than normal.

She twisted without complaint, and my hands worked their way from her hips, enjoying the flinches she made as I did so until I grasped her tits and squeezed. Her back arched, and I leaned down to suck on her neck.

"Roman," she moaned.

"I've got you," I whispered in her ear before grabbing the soap. If I didn't get her clean then, there would be no chance of it happening later.

Bubbles formed in my hands as she pressed closer. I drew her right leg up first, pulling it back until she began to slide down, and did my best to ignore the bruises there.

Gently, I washed every inch I could reach from our position and moved on to the other leg. By the time I was done with them, she was quivering beneath me, and I'd never been so hard in my life. She tried to turn over and face me, but I stopped her. "Not yet."

My thumb stroked her pouty upper lip as the other hand rubbed the bar of soap over her stomach. Her hands joined mine and guided them over her chest until they were right where she wanted them. The soap fell, and I pinched her nipples until she squirmed above me.

Moving on, I used the remainder of bubbles on my hands to quickly wash her arms before reaching for the shampoo to finish. Rubbing my hands together, I gently massaged her scalp, enjoying the groans of contentment she let out.

"I will never be able to bathe the same again," she groaned, and I couldn't help but chuckle.

"I can't say I'm sorry about that."

"You're trying to ruin me, aren't you?"

I pressed my lips to her shoulder. "I'm treasuring you."

She shuddered, and I nipped at her skin before finishing with the shampoo.

Cait sunk into the water as I helped her rinse the soap out. "Do you feel better?" I asked.

"Depends on your definition of better," she countered.

I got out first and reached for a towel, holding it out toward Cait. She stood, and I appraised the perfection that was her body without shame. Every curve was memorized, every freckle would never be forgotten. Nothing about her was hidden from me, and I was cherishing the moment.

With measured movements, I dried her off and let her do the same to me before picking her up and walking our naked asses back to the bedroom. I laid her out on the bed, running my hands over her smooth skin.

Our connection buzzed with an intensity like never before, and I recalled during the ceremony when I'd been able to hear her thoughts, making me try again.

Kitten? I thought but received nothing in return.

I crawled over Cait, placing one knee on each side of her. Her hips lifted and tempted me, but there would be no sex between us yet. She wasn't ready for it, even if her hormones were saying otherwise. That didn't mean I couldn't love her in other ways, though.

Using my left hand, I pressed her back into the bed before blazing a trail of kisses over her chest until I reached her nipples. Each one was sucked until they peaked just the way I wanted them. Her hands reached for my dick, but it wasn't time for her touches yet.

I gathered her wrists with one hand and placed them above her head. "Stay."

She pouted, but I didn't relent, tightening my grip until she nodded. "Yes, sir."

My dick twitched against her thigh, and Cait grinned as I ventured back down her body. My tongue swirled around her belly button as my hands spread her legs apart, tracing circles over her skin until she wiggled beneath me.

"Roman," she begged.

"Yes?"

"I *need* more."

Pleasuring her was my newest joy, and I wanted to give my mate everything. She had all of my heart, and I'd give her as much of my body as I knew she was ready for.

"Your wish is my command." My head dipped between her legs, and I slowly and torturously dragged my tongue over her folds. Her fingers gripped my hair and pressed me closer as I inhaled her arousal. Adding a finger, I stroked her clit as her hold on me grew and her hips moved in motion with my hand.

Her breathing increased as I picked up speed, pressing harder and flicking my tongue in time with her movements.

"Holy shit," she moaned as her muscles tightened around my finger. I added a second one to lift her higher. She gasped, and her hips jolted up as a smothered scream escaped her lips.

My hand was drenched from her release, but I wasn't done with her yet. No, I planned to love the rest of her body for hours to come.

As she came down from the high, I caressed her skin until she was more coherent. Before I could say anything, she took me by surprise and flipped me over with more strength than I expected. It wasn't with fluid movements by any means, but it was sexy as hell.

"You're not the only one who gets to have fun tonight," she purred.

I raised a brow at her and propped myself up on my elbows. "Are you saying you didn't just have the time of your life?"

"Not at all. Let me rephrase. You're not the only one who gets to do the pleasuring." She shoved me back down with one hand on my chest while the other gripped my dick. "Let's see how long *you* can keep your hands to yourself. The longer you do, the more rewarding it will be."

As her tongue swirled around my hardened tip, I was once again convinced Cait was going to be the death of me, but if this was the way I went out, I'd at least die a happy man.

22

CAIT

I had never been so brazen in my life. There was something about the way Roman's eyes appraised every part of me that gave me the confidence to do things I'd only ever fantasized about.

We fell asleep in a mess of tangled arms and legs sometime in the middle of the night, and considering we didn't actually have sex, I'd never been more sated.

Roman managed to anticipate my every need, and each touch made the connection between us strengthen.

After the ceremony had ended, I'd been worried I had screwed something up and we'd have another problem on our hands, but nothing about the oddities from earlier had been mentioned as we pleasured one another.

Morning had finally arrived, and it was time to come out of our bubble. I knew Roman had been busy making plans while I'd been tortured by Embry, Ramona, and Serene. I had specifically avoided asking about them, because I wasn't ready, but there was no more avoiding.

Roman's fingers traced circles over my stomach. "Good morning, beautiful."

"Good morning indeed." I stretched my sore muscles and inched closer to him, even though I knew we had other things to do.

He groaned, wrapping his arms around my waist. "Shower and then reality?" he suggested.

"Probably a good idea. I'm pretty sure there's still whipped cream where it doesn't belong." Yes, we'd gone there, and yes, it was hot and delicious.

Roman chuckled against my shoulder as he got out of bed and hauled me to the bathroom with him. I side-eyed the tub, remembering how our evening had started. Heat consumed me as I licked my lips.

"We'll have a repeat of that again soon," he said, turning on the shower and leaving his very naked ass on display for my viewing pleasure.

As he leaned forward to adjust the showerheads, I took the opportunity to give his muscled perfection a solid smack. He tensed and growled, then slowly turned back toward me. His azure eyes danced with excitement as he stalked toward me.

Without saying a word, he tossed me over his shoulder and paddled my ass three times with his open palm. "Wash. Now."

"Yes, sir."

He stood in the corner of the shower, using one side while I took the other. Instead of furthering the torture for both of us, I cleaned up as quickly as I could and handed him a towel when we finished.

"Shit. I have no clothes here," I said as I went for the brush I'd seen when I'd been alone in his room before.

"Yes, you do. Also, don't think I didn't notice the presents you left behind yesterday morning," he called over his shoulder as he confidently strode naked back into the bedroom.

I grinned while brushing my hair. Roman returned already dressed in jeans and holding a pair of women's shorts, underwear, and a green tank top. "I like this color on you," he said.

I eyeballed the items suspiciously. "These aren't mine."

"Yes, they are. I bought them for you. Like that brush you're using. Did you not think I'd be prepared for my mate once I found you?"

My chest twinged and throat burned with emotion. I didn't deserve him yet, but hopefully one day I would.

His thumbs stroked my cheeks, wiping away a stray tear. "Everything is new and yours. Anything you don't want can be donated."

I nodded, and he pressed his lips to my forehead. "Now get ready. We have things to discuss with the others."

I raised a brow, trying not to let nerves ruin my mood. "Like what? Did something happen?"

"Not at the moment, but it's time to put everything on the table and decide what we intend to do about the things we've learned. I haven't forgotten what Cohen did. He will pay for taking you. Plus, what it means that you're here. Between what Beatrix said and the Moon Goddess, we need a plan in place to keep you safe."

As much as I appreciated his obvious care, he had his thoughts headed in the wrong direction.

"Roman, you can't keep me safe."

His chest rumbled, the sound echoing against the bathroom walls. "Excuse me?"

"I mean, you can, but that's not what is going to happen." I waved a hand over myself. "I didn't become this new me to be hidden away. I was created for a purpose. What I can do, it's meant to help people."

During one of our brief intermissions the night before, he'd finally asked about the bruises, and I'd filled him in on what new abilities I'd learned.

His head shook. "I won't risk you."

I grabbed both of his hands. "I fought this new world when I first got here because I was scared of the unknown, but when I… was reborn, I made a choice to not live in fear. I won't run from whatever is coming. We need to fight."

"I don't like it," he said through clenched teeth.

"Neither do I, but we don't have a choice."

"Yes, we do. I could kill anyone that looks at you wrong."

I laughed. "No, you can't."

"I can," he challenged.

I shoved a finger in his chest. "Okay, you can, but no killing unless we have no other choice."

He pouted, and I knew I'd won. "I don't like your rules."

"You're just mad because they're better than yours."

Roman rested his forehead on mine. "I will keep you safe."

"I know, but there's a reason I am what I am. It's time to find that out. Even if we don't like it," I replied.

Luna, the Moon Goddess, had said some cryptic words when she'd saved me, but a part of me had shoved that information aside, trying to pretend things weren't as screwed up as they seemed. We'd had our fun. There was no more room for pretending I hadn't been created to fight something bigger than myself.

It took more effort than I expected to step away from Roman. "Finish getting dressed. Like you said, we have things to discuss, and we'll get nowhere staying in this bedroom."

He grinned. "I'd say we got plenty accomplished last night."

"Not the point." I gave him a push toward the door. "Let me finish getting ready."

Roman bowed. "As you wish, Mate."

The way "mate" rolled off his tongue so fluidly made my skin tingle. I was beginning to understand what Embry and Ramona had meant when they'd told me having a mate was a gift. A part of me wished I'd been born into this world, so I'd have known better before, but at the same time, it made things more interesting to learn and grow with Roman at my side.

I didn't want to waste time blow-drying my hair, so

I towel-dried and called it good before moving on to brushing teeth and moisturizing.

Roman was waiting for me when I finished, and he seemed just as tense as before. Something told me this was going to be a new normal for him for the foreseeable future.

He opened his hand to me, and I gladly took it as he led me downstairs. "The others are already waiting for us in the conference room."

"Oh! Can I do the mind-talk now?" I asked, mentally kicking myself for not thinking about that earlier.

"I tried to reach out to you last night, but you didn't respond. I'm hoping it comes in time," he said, and my shoulders drooped.

Well, that wasn't what I wanted to hear.

We walked into the meeting room to find Embry, Vaughn, Sam, Ramona, and Jack waiting for us. A blush covered my cheeks as Embry waggled her eyebrows at me, but thankfully she didn't say anything that would have had me plotting her death.

"Good morning, everyone," Roman said as he pulled a chair out for me next to his at the head of the table.

Greetings went around the table as we got settled. "Let's get straight to it with what we know," Roman began. "Our top priorities are bringing Cohen down once and for all, figuring out why Cait's path was sped up, and finding out who we can trust."

"The list of those we can count on is going to be a lot

shorter than the one made up of people we can't. Word is already traveling about what happened in Sydney, but nobody knows Cait's name. They're calling her the Lavender Wolf in the chat boards," Sam said first.

Lavender Wolf. I wasn't a fan, but it could have been worse.

"Was my name mentioned?" Roman asked, and Sam nodded. "Then, it doesn't matter if they know Cait's name. They know enough. Where are we with security around the pack, Vaughn?"

"More sensors have gone up and shifts have been extended. All wolves currently on rotation have volunteered to be there, and I'm receiving no push back."

Roman nodded stiffly. "I know Serene isn't normally part of these meetings, but I expected her to be here. Does anyone know if she's heard anything more from Beatrix?"

"Beatrix won't be assisting us anymore. She already did more than expected. Her coven needs her at the moment," Ramona answered.

"She said Cait was going to balance out what was broken. Does anyone believe that's going to apply outside of the issues we have with Cohen? Is this bigger than we know in a way that will affect our pack directly?"

Sam leaned back in her seat, taking a casual pose, but the tone of her voice was anything but calm. "I keep a lot of what I do to myself for good reason. Most of my assignments are too dark for even supernaturals to handle. Things have only gotten progressively worse over the last few months. When Lucinda left L.A. for Fae Islands, some of the supes in the area began to push boundaries the snarky fae had made. This was only the beginning."

"The beginning of what?" Embry asked.

"Nobody knows, and that's the problem. Things are changing at a rapid pace. Witches are gathering and going underground. Vampires are creating newborns as if they expect a mass culling. Fae have left their realm, though they are slowly going back. What we've always known about our secret world is no more," Sam answered.

"How do I fit into all of that?" I asked, not wanting to be a bystander in something that had so much to do with me.

"That's the golden question, isn't it?" Sam said.

"So, nobody knows what's happening, only that something is. Then, where do we start?" Vaughn asked.

"We start with Cohen. I want him dealt with first, so we don't have to worry about his underhandedness on top of everything else. He came for Cait once, and when he learns she's still alive, he'll do it again," Roman answered, no surprise to me. He'd wanted his grandfather's blood since the moment he got me back.

"I have something to say," Ramona said and stood with Jack at her side.

All eyes went to them.

"We spent a lot of time thinking about this and

believe it's the best choice," Ramona said once they had everyone's attention.

"What choice would that be?" Roman asked.

"My father has longed for a life he wasn't destined for. Nothing has ever been good enough for him, because he's never deserved better than what he got. Before I left him, he vowed to find a way to become the ultimate wolf, one capable of rivaling the council. I'd always ignored his ramblings, but I believe we need to consider him a more formidable opponent this time around," Ramona answered.

"Why do you think that?" Sam asked.

"I've been thinking about what Cait went through. He had her exactly where he wanted, then let her go. Cohen is a lot of things, but mostly, he's a control freak. He wouldn't have initiated taking her without having thought every step through."

My gut twisted as Ramona spoke.

"Cohen let her go," Embry said.

Roman slammed his fist on the table. "No, he let that witch kill her."

"Yes, that, too. But maybe he knew Cait needed to walk a certain path before he could use her," Ramona added.

"How could he know that?" Vaughn asked.

"That is the question we need to answer first," Jack said. "We need to find out what Cohen knows before he makes his next move."

My eyes went to Roman as I began to figure out what "choice" Ramona and Jack thought was best.

Roman sat straight up in his chair, shoulders tight and jaw locked. On instinct, I moved closer to him and grabbed his hand, knowing he wasn't going to handle what came next well.

"How do we figure that out?" Sam asked.

Jack and Ramona shared a look before she spoke. "We're going to their pack to live for as long as it takes to do so."

Roman's head snapped toward his mother. "Like hell you are."

23

CAIT

Ramona narrowed her eyes. "That's not your choice to make, Son."

He stood slowly, placing his palms on top of the table, and sneered at her. "I'm not only your son. I'm your alpha, and if I say you're to stay on these pack lands, then that's exactly what you'll do."

Oh, shit. I'd never heard him speak to his mother that way, and I had no idea how Ramona was about to handle the situation she'd created.

"Don't overstep your power, Roman. If you'd listen to reason, you would know this is the best choice," she said.

"Putting any of you at risk is never the best choice. I won't allow it."

Jack nodded at Ramona before she spoke again. "Then, you leave us with no choice. We'd like to be released from the pack."

Gasps sounded from every person in the room

except the three of them. I had no idea what it truly meant to be released, but I knew there couldn't be anything good about it.

"You'd really disrespect me like that?" Roman asked, voice low and lethal.

"If you refuse to let me do what I know is best, then you leave me no choice," Ramona answered, never once wavering in her confidence.

Roman straightened. "You're putting me in an impossible situation."

"We're only trying to help. After speaking with you and Vaughn, I knew there wasn't much choice and your mother agreed. We won't let you go after Cohen on a whim. He's smarter than you're giving him credit for, and we won't lose you," Jack said.

"If that was the case, then you'd stay," Roman sneered before regaining control of himself. "I won't release you. Not back to Cohen."

"That's not what we're asking," Ramona said.

"Then, to who?" Sam asked first, suddenly more intrigued than seemed appropriate.

Jack glanced at his niece. "To ourselves."

Roman laughed, the sound sinister. "You've lost your damn mind. That's not happening."

"We'll leave with or without your permission, Son. You can't hold two alphas where they don't want to be. Cohen will be too tempted to pass up the opportunity to have Ramona in his pack. She can get close to him and make him pay, but not before finding out what his plans are," Jack said.

Roman pointed at both of them. "Out of all the people in the world, I never expected the two of you would be the ones to turn on me."

"We're not turning on anyone," Ramona replied, and I could finally see how much this conversation was costing her emotionally.

"Yes, you are. You're not willing to find another way to get the information we need. You're being selfish."

His mother smiled, the gesture filled with sadness. "One day, you'll see that's the opposite of what's happening."

"We love you, Son. We'll let you think about what we've said and revisit it tomorrow, but we won't wait longer than that to see how easy or difficult our choice will be," Jack said, then he and Ramona left the room while the rest of us sat there, stunned.

"I'm going to go talk to them," Sam said.

Roman snarled at her. "No. They've made their choice."

"Don't be an idiot, Ro. I know you're hurting, but they aren't making this choice to spite you."

She got up, and Roman didn't stop her from walking out as well.

"Sam is right. I don't agree with the way they went about things, but they're your parents and they love you," Vaughn said as he got up and pulled Embry with him.

My best friend glanced at me and raised a brow, but I shook my head. I wasn't going to leave Roman. He needed someone in his corner. While I knew the rest of them were giving him space to wrap his head around the situation, I was confident that wasn't what he needed from me.

Once the room was empty and the door closed, I stood and turned him toward me. "Fear is something I've lived with since the moment my mom died. It has taken more from me than I'd like to admit, and I don't want it to do the same to you," I said to him.

"I can't lose them. I can't lose any of you," he replied, gathering me into his arms.

His hold on me was suffocating, but I returned the gesture just as tightly.

Energy swirled inside me as we stood together, unmoving and silent.

"I can fix this," he finally said.

"How?"

"By killing Cohen before my parents can get there. I'll leave tonight and be back before morning."

I was hopeful he was only thinking his thoughts out loud with no intention of acting on them. Rushing into the West Texas pack wasn't the smartest move and deep down, he knew that.

"Whatever you have to do, I will back you, but your plans need to be well thought-out," I said.

"Even if they make me a murderer?"

"I'll help you bury the body. Just be smart about this. I can't lose you, either." I smiled softly, hoping to lighten the mood, but it didn't work.

He held me tighter. "I don't ever want you—"

Roman's words cut off mid-sentence, and he went rigid in my arms. I took a step back. "What's wrong?"

"They're here."

"Who?"

"Cohen, Kyle, Callista, and too many members of his pack."

I grabbed his hand and headed for the door, but Roman jerked me back. "You're not going out there."

"I know you're scared, but I promise I can handle this. We can do this together," I said before silently reaching out to Adira. *Can't we?*

If you believe we can, then yes, she replied.

She'd been abnormally quiet lately, but I'd begun to learn that the more I did things right, the more she was just along for the ride.

"You'll stay with me the entire time and you won't object if I ask you to go for your own safety," Roman said, already moving in front of me to lead the way.

"I won't put myself at risk," I agreed, but not necessarily to what he wanted.

"Then, let's run."

We raced down the hallway and out the door only to find men, women, and wolves alike all fighting with each other. I had no idea how this had happened so quickly, but there was no time to question it.

Roman continued forward as I searched for Embry, catching her pink hair disappearing and her wolf clawing her way into the fight.

Power pulsed inside me, and my skin began to glow. The connection between Roman and me grew stronger and he glanced back at me, his own eyes taking on a purple hue.

We might not have been bonded, but there was something growing between us, and I wasn't mad about it.

"Shift," he demanded as I witnessed him grow taller and wider before my eyes. Though, I was surprised he didn't change into his wolf.

My animal form was the easiest to fight in, because she was quicker than I could be on two feet, so I didn't hesitate at his request. The transformation came faster than ever before, and I felt taller than normal, too. My head was well above Roman's waistline.

A wolf lunged for me, and Adira was fully present, twisting us out of the way and sinking her teeth into the rear flank of our attacker. She moved quicker than I could follow, ripping out a chunk of hair and skin from the opposing wolf along the way.

Roman stepped between us, but it wasn't necessary.

I leaped around him, vibrating with energy that needed to be expelled. I landed on top of the wolf, not giving him a chance to get away, and bit into his neck until he relaxed beneath my hold. I wasn't there to kill anyone if I didn't have to, but I had no problem putting someone in their place.

Except this wolf wasn't having any of that. As soon as I'd thought he was going to comply and stand down, he kicked me in the gut, and my wolf went several yards in the air. Roman moved to help, and I cut him off a second time. I needed my mate to see what he hadn't yet. I was capable of more than he knew.

Using my friction power, I sped forward and rammed into the side of the other wolf. He yelped and went soaring into a tree, landing limp at the bottom. I wasn't sure if he was dead or knocked out, but there was no time to care.

Adira trotted us back over to Roman who seemed a bit less frazzled and nodded at us. "I won't be missing any more of your trainings," was all he said before we moved on, heading in a specific direction.

Any idea what the plan is? I asked to Adira, but it wasn't her that answered.

I'm going to kill Cohen before he hurts my mother, Roman's voice sounded.

Well, we might not have been able to mind-speak earlier, but whatever magic I seemed to be sharing with Roman at the moment had changed that.

I focused on where Roman was headed and spotted a limping wolf fighting with an all-black one while Ramona went hand-to-hand with her sperm donor.

"Help my father," Roman said as we got closer, and I began to put the situation together. Kyle had to be the black wolf and Jack was the one not able to hold his own. The exact reason Roman had taken over for him.

Moving away from Roman, I took a wider path around in hopes of sneaking up on Kyle as I started to channel my spirit wolf form. Just as I began to creep closer, a dark chill ran down my spine.

I checked behind me, but nobody was paying me

any attention. Continuing on, I lowered myself to the ground and called every ounce of power I could muster. I might not have been muscle strong, but my energy packed a punch. One I planned to introduce to Kyle.

Jumping into the air, I hit an invisible wall and crashed to the ground as energy was sucked from me, causing me to lose the spirit form that kept me safest.

Shift back! Adira yelled at me, and I did so without question.

As soon as I was on two feet, I turned around to find Callista standing behind me. "You're going to wish you'd stayed dead the first time I killed you."

"I don't think I will." I grinned at her and took a step forward, knowing exactly what I had planned for her. Spirit wolf or not, this bitch wouldn't kill me a second time.

24

CAIT

Callista still had a scar down her cheek from our last fight, and I planned to give her several more. I briefly wondered if Cohen planned to kill the witch when she was no longer useful. Considering she was standing before me, he still needed her for something, and I had every intention of putting her out of service before that happened.

I had nothing to say to the witch. After hearing the theory that Cohen had intentionally let me go, that they'd killed me in order to turn me into what I was... Well, I was going to show them what a mistake that was on their part.

If you're in wolf form, she's going to try to siphon your magic. Be careful with your next moves, Adira said.

Got it.

Callista circled her hands around, dark blue magic forming between her palms. She shoved them outward, sending the swirls at me. I dodged to the left, but she still managed to singe my arm. The sensation felt like stabbing needles that were spreading at a leisurely pace. I glanced down and let out several choice words.

The midnight-colored magic was traveling over my arm in a slow, expanding circle while the feeling in my fingers was fading.

Embry's wolf crashed into the barrier Callista had put up. "It's just you and me, wolf," the witch taunted.

I should have been nervous, but instead, I was just pissed the hell off. Adira had warned me not to shift, which made things harder than I liked. I tried to draw on my spirit form again, but whatever cage Callista stuck us in was blocking some of my abilities.

Before I could re-evaluate my situation, she struck first, harder than I'd been prepared for. I had to think on my feet and put my next moves into motion without wasting time I didn't have.

My shoulder drooped as I stumbled. "What did you do to me?"

"Just a bit of paralyzing magic concocted just for you."

She stepped closer and circled me as I increased my breathing, pretending to swat at her and acting weaker than I felt.

Embry howled, a painful sound to my ears. She didn't know what I was up to, but it was better this way. Adira had taught me early that an opponent almost always thought they had the upper hand until they didn't. I was going to use this against Callista, because there wasn't a single part of me that believed the witch was scared of me.

"Your death might teach them all a lesson, but not before I take everything that makes you a shifter away," Callista stated.

"I never wanted it anyway," I replied.

She laughed and shoved me to the ground. "So pathetic. You'd choose death over the powerful life you could have had if you'd only known what you were capable of."

Oh, I knew enough, and she was about to get a front row seat to my show. I just had to cross my fingers that I wasn't wrong about the extent of my power while in this magical cage.

I rested my face in the ground, my hair creating a curtain over my eyes. Callista kneeled next to me. "You had more backbone when you were human."

"No, I just acted without thinking before," I said before latching on to her wrist with my good arm and bringing my wolf power forward. I tied myself to Callista using the friction energy, my hold unyielding as I drew on my magic hard and fast.

I'd never called the energy forward in this way before, but with a clear head, I had high hopes it would do what I wanted.

Callista screeched like a banshee in my ear while trying her best to back away. When that didn't work, she grabbed the hair at the base of my neck and slammed my face into the ground with enough force to break my nose.

Still, I kept my hold on her and the friction energy covered my body, heating me from the inside out while I pushed the magic away from me, willing it to do my bidding.

Be careful, Cait, Adira warned.

Something I'd learned while figuring out what I was capable of was that things always worked best when I followed my instincts and didn't overthink what I needed to do. I was treating this situation no differently.

Whatever happened to me would be worth it as long as Callista ceased to exist. She needed to pay for killing me.

Callista wasn't giving up easily. When I moved to sit up so she couldn't smash my face into the dirt again, she began to mutter words under her breath, and her dark eyes took on a silver glow just like the witches in Sydney had.

The magic I was pushing into her began to move faster, but not because I wanted it to. Just like Adira had said, Callista was trying to siphon my power. I'd give her only enough to finish what I started.

I caught an elbow to the jaw as I stood us both up. Her dark magic intertwined with my purple, creating a tornado of energy that would have been striking to watch under different circumstances.

With my dominant arm still gripping her wrist, I used my near useless arm to grab her neck. *I need your strength, Adira.*

My wolf rose to the surface, giving me exactly what I asked for. I pushed Callista back toward the ground, so she kneeled before me. "You can't beat me. You're nothing other than a vessel for magic you don't deserve," she spat with shaky limbs.

I didn't justify her words with a response. That would only have given her what she wanted. Instead, I overpowered the pull she had on me and found a way past whatever blocks she'd had up. The moment I sensed the energy change, I transformed into my spirit form. Her eyes turned into slits as her chin jutted up.

The witch was ready for her death. That almost made me want to leave her alive, but someone like her would never stop coming for me. She needed to be dealt with properly before she hurt anyone else.

Beads of sweat began to form on her forehead as I pushed harder, increasing my friction energy while holding on to my spirit form that prevented her from hurting me. I had every intention of frying the bitch to a crisp, and I was well on my way until she snapped her fingers and the cage that she'd magicked around us fell.

Noise of the fighting around us increased, and a wolf slammed into my side, sending me flying in the wrong direction and breaking the hold I'd had on Callista, along with all of my concentration.

When I landed and twisted around, Kyle's black wolf was circling Callista protectively, licking his lips and snapping at me.

"You can't hurt me," I said as I got up and shifted into my own wolf with the intention of using the spirit form as well, but every time I tried, nothing happened.

I was losing steam after letting Callista take power

from me, but Adira was ready. Kyle ran for us, and she leaped over him, landing next to Callista, who was groaning on the ground after what I'd put her through. I might not be burning her insides anymore, but I'd taken more of her energy than she'd realized.

I can kill her now, Adira said.

Then, do it, I replied.

Glancing back at Kyle who was getting closer, Adira snarled at him and moved so we were still next to Callista and facing the approaching wolf before we made our move.

With snapping jaws, Adira bit down on the witch's neck and twisted her head back and forth. When the witch's blood began to fill my wolf's mouth, we dropped her to the ground. Callista's head was nearly severed off, and I felt confident there was no coming back from that injury for the witch before I refocused on Kyle.

I wasn't quick enough, though.

Kyle's wolf landed on top of us, and his front claws dug into the underbelly of my wolf until they broke skin. He bit into our shoulder as his nails ripped our stomach open.

I called my energy forward again but remembered Callista's paralyzing magic. Between all I'd already done and the dark magic working its way through me, I was too exhausted. Even Adira had trouble fighting back, which only meant one thing given our current situation.

We were going to bleed out, and there wasn't a damn thing left in me to do anything about it.

Kyle stood above us and howled in success, but the sounds that followed assured only his death for daring to touch me.

I'm coming, Cait.

Roman's voice was a promise that came just a moment too late.

25

ROMAN

As soon as I spotted Cohen, six wolves descended on me. He wasn't man enough to face me himself and thought I could be beat by a half-dozen poorly trained beasts. Well, I wouldn't let him come to my pack and hurt my family. Nothing would stop me from showing him the consequences of his choices.

With my focus on the wolves and making sure Cohen didn't run away like a coward, I'd lost track of Cait, but I could still feel our connection, so I didn't let the fact I couldn't see her distract me.

One wolf after another, I tossed them aside as if they were nothing. I'd never felt more capable, and I knew I had Cait to thank for that.

By the time I finished with the distractions Cohen sent to me, he was holding my mother in his arms, and his hand was partially shifted. His claws dug into my mom's neck, but there was no fear in her eyes.

She was prepared to die for me, but I wasn't going to let that happen.

"Let her go," I roared.

"I don't think I will. She's *my* daughter, after all," Cohen countered.

"She hasn't been anything to you since the day you tried to keep her from her true mate."

His hold sank deeper, drawing blood. "She was *my* heir. Now I have none, which means I had to come up with another plan. One that will allow me to rule for years to come."

"And you thought my mate would help you get that? You won't ever get your hands on her again," I said.

Cohen laughed and nodded behind me. "Oh, boy. You're so young and naïve. Callista is taking care of her now for me."

Taking a chance that he wasn't lying, I turned back. My mate was on the ground, but I could feel her energy pulsing with plenty of life. She'd asked me to trust her, to believe she was capable. Instead of abandoning my mother, I did as Cait had asked, and hoped like hell I wouldn't regret my choice.

"Seems to me your witch would rather see Cait dead. I don't see how that's helpful to you," I said.

"Dead or alive. It doesn't matter to me as long as I get her magic. Her kind is what our world needs, and I'm going to show everyone why."

I met my mom's stare. She was one of the bravest women I'd ever known. Nothing scared her, and dying at the hands of her own father was no different. She nodded at me, giving me permission to do whatever it took to end this.

Except before I could act, I was reminded that Cait had never made it to my dad. Kyle stomped over my father's broken wolf, blood coating his muzzle and a spark in his eyes that meant nothing good.

"At least someone around here knows how to do what he's told," Cohen muttered, forcing my mother to look. "You chose wrong. I could have made you into something great, and now you're left with nothing."

"You can take it all away from me and I'll still have more in this world than you could ever understand," my mother said as tears finally fell down her cheeks.

No, this was not how things ended for my parents. I wouldn't let it happen. I shifted to my wolf form and leapt for Cohen. He hadn't expected me to go for him. He likely assumed I'd have avenged my father, but that could come next. I needed to save my mother.

Cohen shoved his daughter to the ground and began to shift, except something wasn't working right. His wolf form wasn't taking shape like normal. Cohen had either messed with too much dark magic, or his wolf was fighting him. Either way, I intended to use that to my advantage.

I bit down on his leg and sank both of my front paws into his stomach. Dark magic filtered out of Cohen's exposed wounds, explaining why he couldn't shift properly into his wolf. He'd gone down a path not even his other half could agree with.

Cohen kicked me in the gut, throwing me off of him, but I didn't lose balance for long. He attacked next, and I was ready for him.

He managed to leave a long scrape down my face, but that wasn't enough to stop me. No, I had too many people counting on me. I had to stop him. I had to protect Cait and my parents and everyone else.

It didn't matter that I shared blood with this man. If anything, that gave me even more reason to kill after all Cohen had done to my family.

We need to hurry. Something is wrong, my wolf said.

With Cait?

I don't know.

That was all I needed to hear to finish what I'd been itching to do ever since I got Cait back. I wouldn't lose her a second time.

My wolf spit and snarled above Cohen's half-shifted form. I worked with my wolf as one, something we'd become quite versed in over the years.

Cohen howled in my ear, but the sound cut off as I tore into his neck. Blood coated my throat as I ripped through his fur and into skin. I continued until I hit bone, then jerked with everything I had. Taking out a wolf's neck was the number one way to kill an opponent. I could have gone for something more dramatic, but I needed to get to Cait more than anything else.

Once his wolf stopped twitching under my hold, I released him and spit as much of his tainted blood out as I could before I glanced at my mother, who was hovered over my father. The other fights around us had dispersed for the most part, but there was still one I had to contend with before I mourned my father.

That pain had to be pushed aside until I knew everyone else was safe.

Turning back toward where Cait was, I had a proud moment as I watched her end Callista. I'd thought this part of the supernatural life would be the hardest for my mate to acclimate to, but she was born to be Luna Marked, and it showed with everything Cait did since the moment she accepted her fate.

As I moved toward her, Kyle closed the distance between him and Cait, landing on top of her, ripping apart her stomach, and tearing a chunk from her shoulder. Crimson mixed with the purple of her wolf, and fury engulfed every inch of me as something resembling a howl ripped from my chest.

I'm coming, Cait, I promised as my wolf's legs ran as fast as they could.

Kyle fled the area, along with the rest of the West Texas wolves. I trusted my own to follow them and focused solely on the shallow breaths of the most important person in the world to me.

I shifted back to human form and crawled to her side. "I'm so sorry, Cait. Stay with me and everything is going to be okay. It has to be."

Her wolf whimpered as I stroked her back. *Can you hear me?*

Roman. Cait's voice was weak, but I chose to focus on the fact she could reply at all.

Embry was behind me. "What can I do?"

"Call a fucking healer."

Cait was never going to heal properly in her wolf form. I'd only ever commanded a wolf's transformation once before, and it didn't go very well, but I had to try now, so we could see the extent of her injuries.

"Shift, Cait. Now," I said, allowing my alpha power to flow through us. More cries sounded from her wolf, further breaking my heart. She wasn't fighting me. Her energy was just too low.

I said SHIFT! I demanded through our connection.

The lavender from Cait's wolf began to darken, and she trembled under my touch. *You can do this,* I encouraged. *I need you to shift.*

Finally, her form shimmered and changed into my perfect mate. Cait was covered in blood and naked, something I normally would have been bothered by, but ignored for the time being.

Serene appeared next to me as I turned to see if Embry had gone to find a healer as I'd asked. "Use this." The historian shoved a bottle of green liquid toward me.

"What is it?" I snapped.

"Something Beatrix left. I'm not sure what exactly, but she said to use it under a life-or-death circumstance. I'd consider this one of those given all the blood covering the ground mixed with dark magic."

The old wolf was right. Beatrix had been helpful thus far, and I was growing desperate as Cait's heart rate slowed to dangerous levels. The shift had taken more effort than she had to give. Even our bond couldn't fix the visible wounds, and who knew what else was damaged on the inside.

"I'm so sorry, Cait," I whispered as I opened the vial.

She murmured incoherently as I opened her mouth. The liquid sloshed around until she nearly choked, and I was forced to hold her lips closed until she could swallow. The actions felt wrong, but I was left with no other choice.

Coldness surrounded me as Cait's chest expanded, and she sucked in a deep breath. Her back arched, and a toe-curling scream tore from her. One of my fists slammed into the dirt as I waited for her green eyes to stare up at me, confirming everything was going to be okay.

Her arms stayed glued to her sides as if they weighed a hundred pounds each. I gripped her shoulders. "Cait!"

She didn't respond, and her skin burned me with how icy it was.

"What's wrong with her?" I yelled at Serene.

"Just wait."

I snarled. "Wait for what? My mate to *die*? I don't fucking think so."

Embry nudged me. "Look."

My attention focused where Embry pointed. Cait's breathing started to level out, and her heartbeat thrummed in time with my own. I held her hands, still freezing, but they began to warm with my touch. I rubbed my palms over her exposed skin, avoiding the open wounds still seeping with blood that also matted her hair.

"Come on, Mate. I need you to open those perfect eyes for me," I begged as tears fell from my eyes.

Cait's back lowered to the ground, no longer stiff and arched up. I thought that was a good thing until she stopped moving at all.

No heartbeat. No rising of her chest.

Nothing.

There was nothing but her precious body.

Embry's sobs sounded from behind me but were quickly drowned out by a ringing in my ears so loud I thought I'd gone mad. Maybe I had. Without Cait, I had nothing.

I lay my head on her chest, uncaring that her blood now covered me. I wanted to die with her.

Roman.

Her voice was so faint, I assumed it to be my imagination running rampant, but then I heard it again. Stronger this time.

Roman.

"Cait?" I leaned up, brushing her hair back and feeling for a pulse. Still, there was nothing there.

I covered my head with my hands as my shoulders shook. I didn't care that I cried in front of my pack. Cait might have only been my mate for a short time, but I already knew I'd never be able to live without her.

My heart would never beat the same, and as soon as I ripped Kyle's from his chest, I'd find a way to be with her again.

I heard a gasp, then a choking cough.

"Oh, my God." Embry's shocked tone had me opening my eyes.

Cait was trying to roll over, and she was choking on her own blood.

"I got you, Cait. Just breathe for me," I said, trying not to lose my shit as my emotions experienced the worst roller coaster of my life.

"Ro—" she stammered and coughed.

"Shhh. I'm right here."

Her wounds began to close right before my eyes, something not normal even for supernaturals. Still, I was afraid to move her more than necessary.

She opened her eyes, gasping at all the blood. "Did I die again?"

"I don't know. If you didn't, it was damn close," I growled.

"I'm sorry I'm naked again," she said, voice growing stronger by the second.

I laughed as the last of my tears dried up. Her words were so unexpected and needed, all at the same time. "That is the least of my worries right now."

She tried to sit up, but I softly held her down. "Let's give you another few minutes."

Cait nodded, and as much as I feared looking away from her, I had to search for my mother. "Where are my parents?"

"Sam is with them and the healer I called for," Embry answered.

"The healer? Is my mom hurt?" I assumed my father

was already dead and was too afraid to hope for otherwise.

She shook her head. "Jack is barely hanging on, but he has a chance. Ramona got to him just in time to slow the bleeding."

My head tilted back as I silently thanked the Moon Goddess for so many different things.

"Can I get up now?" Cait asked. Her words began to slow as exhaustion set in.

"No, but I will carry you." I scooped her up as gently as possible.

For the first time, I took in the sight of our front yard and driveway. Too much blood and too many bodies lay on the ground, causing another fissure to run through my heart. I'd promised my pack I'd do whatever I could to keep the fight away from our front door and that was exactly where it had ended up.

Cohen and Callista might be dead, but Kyle wasn't. He'd run away like a coward, and as soon as Cait was back to perfect, I would hunt him down.

I'm going to eat his heart for dessert, my wolf said earnestly.

And I'm going to tear his head from his body, I replied while I held a now-sleeping Cait close to my chest.

As I headed back to the pack house to let Cait rest, Vaughn's wolf came speeding toward me. He leaped and shifted in mid-air, bowing his head. "He got away."

"Kyle can run as far as he wants. He'll never get far enough to hide from me," I said, and added, "Thank you."

Vaughn nodded. "Is Cait okay?"

"She will be." I looked around once more. "I'll be back in a few minutes to help."

"Take care of her. I have this," Vaughn replied.

I shook my head. "My father. He's not in a good place."

"Damn it!" Vaughn ran a bloodied hand through his hair, nearly as furious I was on the inside. "We're going to get them all. Every single wolf that was here."

"Yes, we will," I agreed, then shifted Cait as she groaned in my arms.

Vaughn moved on as I went to the house. Cait didn't need to see the destruction left behind. She'd have enough dark shit to sort through when she was fully coherent.

By the time we got up to my room, she was passed out again, but her heartbeat was strong and her breathing steady. I absolutely did not want to leave her, but I needed to see my parents.

Embry? I called for her, and a knock sounded at my door as it opened.

"I'm already here. I'll let you know if she wakes up or if anything changes," Embry said.

I clasped my hand over her shoulder. "Thank you. Are you okay?"

"I'm fine."

I could sense she wasn't, but Embry was a strong wolf, and if she needed help, I trusted her to say so. I kissed Cait's forehead. "I'll be back as soon as I can." Then, I walked away before I changed my mind.

26

CAIT

Vicious dreams assaulted my sleep. Skies covered in crimson. Dead wolves. Cries of sorrow. They were all never ending, and I couldn't wake. My mind was stuck in the torture for what felt like days.

Pressure pushed down on my chest. The touch light, but persistent.

"I can feel your heart, Cait. It belongs to me. I just need you to wake up. I need *you*." Roman's voice finally broke through the haze my mind had been locked in. The first welcome sound I'd had since I'd fallen asleep.

I tried to do as he asked. I wanted to see his face more than anything, but I couldn't, no matter how hard I tried.

"We buried my father today. There have been burials the last three days, and more are still to come. I can't do another one alone. I can't stand the vacant look in my mother's eyes, because I'm afraid I'm going to know exactly how she feels if you don't wake up."

His voice was hoarse, and his pain seared itself into my heart. He needed me, and I needed him.

I felt his head settle onto my stomach as he held my hands. Awareness was coming back, but not quickly enough. I had to let him know I was there, that I hadn't left him. Not again.

His warmth enveloped me, and I drew on the energy like a lifeline. I used our connection to fuel my drive to fully wake up. Every ounce I pulled into me was like lightning crashing into my body. I had no idea what had happened to me, but I was weaker than I'd ever been, even as a human.

My toes finally moved under the heavy blanket, and I cheered inside my head. I was doing it.

I'm here, Roman. I'm so sorry.

His weight lifted from my torso. "Cait?"

I'm okay. I'm trying to wake up.

Fuck, Cait.

His strangled voice broke me, and I felt the tears pool in my eyes as he gathered me into his arms.

Are you still hurt? he asked.

I don't think so. Don't let go of me.

Not ever.

Roman's fingers brushed over my face. "Don't cry. Everything is going to be fine."

He had no idea I'd heard what he'd said about his dad. Nothing was fine, and as I regained my strength, the last of my memories flashed through my mind. Remembering the fight with Callista, killing her, and then not being able to fight off Kyle. He'd gotten to me when I'd been weighed down by the witch's dark magic. A cheap shot from an unworthy wolf.

Cold vengeance filled me.

My ire broke the last of the hold over me, and I reached for Roman. "I'm so sorry," I sobbed against him while sorrow and rage fought for control over my emotions.

"This wasn't your fault. You have nothing to be sorry for," he murmured into my hair while his fingers stroked every inch of me that they could reach.

"We're going to kill him. He only got to me because Callista hit me with dark magic that prevented me from being able to move as fluidly as normal. If it hadn't been for Adira, I wouldn't have been able to even fight her off."

"Adira?"

I shrugged. "It's the name I call my wolf."

He seemed to think about that for a moment, then moved on. "Do you remember waking up right after I had you shift back?"

I thought about that and couldn't recall anything after Kyle tore into me. "No. Maybe I will later."

Roman grimaced. "You were in a lot of pain. It might be better if you don't."

I reached up and cupped his cheek. "I'm fine now, though."

"Thank the gods for that." His lips pressed to mine, and I practically melted into him. Energy zipped through me as he pressed closer. "I missed you so fucking much," he whispered.

"I heard you mention your father just now. I'm so sorry, Roman. I'd tried to go to him, but—" He covered my mouth.

"His death is not your fault. There is only one person to blame, and I plan to kill him very soon."

I nodded, knowing it was what Roman needed. "What can I do?"

"You waking up is more than enough," he said as Vaughn stormed into the room, holding a piece of paper.

"What's wrong?" Roman asked, tightening his hold on me.

"The council. They've requested Cait's presence." Vaughn shook the letter in his hand, and Roman leaned over to take it.

I tried to read the words, but he angled them away from me. "What does it say?" I asked.

Roman stared at Vaughn, ignoring my question. "This isn't from the wolf council."

"No," Vaughn said, glancing between the two of us.

Roman looked down at me. "I won't let you go to them. They can't have you."

"Who?" My brain wasn't fully understanding why they were freaking out.

"The supernatural council. They've been collecting beings with unusual power. Sam never got to finish telling us what she was trying to figure out. We know now," Roman answered.

"They want to use me?" I asked.

He shook his head. "No, they want to cage you and experiment with your power."

A fire lit inside me, and my wolf howled for the first time since I woke.

I won't be contained, Adira declared.

No, we won't. If they want our power, they're going to have to take it from our dead body.

Agreed.

My eyes met Roman's. "We're not running from this. How do we beat them?"

"We hunt the bastards until there are none of them left."

"Sounds like fun. When do we leave?"

I might have possibly just died for a second time, but I would never be a victim. I was going to keep control of my life. I was going to live my new life how I wanted. Not for, or because of, anyone else.

I was Luna Marked, and it was time to let the supernatural world know what that meant.

///

Join my reader group Heather Renee's Book Warriors to chat all things Luna Marked and to learn more about my other books!

Also, don't forget to preorder Wolf Mated, the final book in the Luna Marked trilogy, releasing Fall 2021!

PS:

Was this book the first time you've met Lucinda? Don't miss out on getting to know her more in my Broken Court series—now complete and available in ebook, paperback, and audio!

STAY IN TOUCH

Find Heather on Facebook:
Reader Group:
Heather Renee's Book Warriors

Author Page:
Heather Renee Author

Or by signing up for her newsletter:
http://smarturl.it/HeatherReneeNL

ABOUT THE AUTHOR

Heather Renee is a *USA Today* bestselling author who lives in Oregon. She writes urban fantasy and paranormal romance novels with a mixture of adventure, humor, and sass. Her love of reading eventually led to her passion for writing and giving the gift of escapism.

When Heather's not writing, she is spending time with her loving husband and beautiful daughter, going on their own adventures. For more ways to connect with her, visit www.HeatherReneeAuthor.com.

ALSO BY HEATHER RENEE

Luna Marked

A wolf shifter series (dual POV) featuring a strong-willed leading lady and a patient, yet fierce alpha male.

Broken Court

A complete Urban Fantasy series featuring an unconventional and anti-heroine leading lady, a broody love interest, and a fae kingdom with a vile king.

Royal Fae Guardians

A complete Urban Fantasy series featuring fae, magic users, a sweet romance, along with snark and humor.

Shadow Veil Academy

A complete Urban Fantasy Academy series featuring shifters, elves, witches, and more.

Elite Supernatural Trackers

A complete Urban Fantasy series featuring witches, demons, a smart-mouthed female lead, alpha males, and a snarky fairy sidekick.

Raven Point Pack Series

A complete Paranormal Romance series featuring wolves, witches, vengeance, and fated mates.

Blood of the Sea Series

A complete Paranormal Romance series featuring vampires, open seas adventures, and the occasional pirate.

Standalone

Marked Paradox - A complete Fantasy fae story about a realm divided and one fae to bring them back together.